Wh

"What I want, Miss ... sheriff said.

Swallowing back her surprise, Julia retorted, "Call me Julia."

"Okay, Julia, we need to talk."

Julia could understand how a criminal would be intimidated by this man. Eric Butler stood almost six feet tall, and right now he was all business. "I'm not sure I understand," she said, wondering if he'd already found out about her late husband's mysterious death. Had he also found out something that would incriminate her? "What do we need to discuss?"

Eric took two long strides toward her. "I want you to tell me why that man would have come to Wildflower... looking for you."

"I didn't know him, if that's what you're asking," Julia replied, praying her daughter would stay put in her room. She didn't want her child to hear this conversation. "I'm telling you the truth."

Eric nodded, then pinned her with another level look. "But did that man happen to know *you?*"

Julia gulped back her fear, her gaze meeting his.

Books by Lenora Worth

Love Inspired Suspense

Fatal Image #38
Secret Agent Minister #68
Deadly Texas Rose #85

Love Inspired

The Wedding Quilt #12
Logan's Child #26
I'll Be Home
  for Christmas #44
Wedding at Wildwood #53
His Brother's Wife #82
Ben's Bundle of Joy #99
The Reluctant Hero #108
One Golden Christmas #122
†*When Love Came*
    to Town #142
†*Something Beautiful* #169

Steeple Hill

After the Storm

†*Lacey's Retreat* #184
‡*The Carpenter's Wife* #211
‡*Heart of Stone* #227
‡*A Tender Touch* #269
A Certain Hope #311
A Perfect Love #330
A Leap of Faith #344
Christmas
  Homecoming #376

†In the Garden
‡Sunset Island
*Texas Hearts

LENORA WORTH

has written more than thirty books, most of those for Steeple Hill Books. She also works freelance for a local magazine, where she had written monthly opinion columns, feature articles and social commentaries. She also wrote for five years for the local paper. Married to her high school sweetheart for thirty-two years, Lenora lives in Louisiana and has two grown children and a cat. She loves to read, take long walks and sit in her garden.

LENORA WORTH

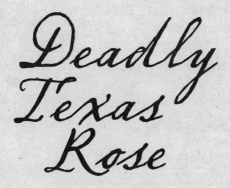

Deadly Texas Rose

Steeple
Hill®

Published by Steeple Hill Books™

STEEPLE HILL BOOKS

Steeple
Hill®

ISBN-13: 978-0-373-44275-1
ISBN-10:   0-373-44275-0

DEADLY ROSE TEXAS

www.SteepleHill.com

Printed in U.S.A.

O that thou wouldest hide me in the grave, that thou wouldest keep me secret, until thy wrath be past, that thou wouldest appoint me a set time, and remember me!

—*Job* 14:13

To Faye Ulmer, everyone's Nana
I love you.

ONE

"Don't move or I'll kill her."

Deputy Sheriff Eric Butler did as he was told, since the mustached stranger standing about five feet away had the new waitress at the Courthouse Café held against her will and a revolver pointed at her head.

"We're all cool here," Eric said, nodding toward all the other customers and the three or four employees who had just minutes before been laughing and talking. "Nobody wants to get hurt today." He silently prayed, asking God to keep everyone safe.

"That's good," the dark-haired, sweating man said, his head bobbing up and down. Then he slanted his gaze around the room where he had ordered the kitchen staff to gather with the customers. In the kitchen, unattended food sizzled and burned on the griddle. "Everybody here, listen to the officer."

Acting on instinct, Eric held his hands away from his body and stared down the shaking man, wondering what kind of idiot would try to rob a restaurant right across from the courthouse in the tiny East-Texas town of Wildflower. Any number of cops and sheriff's deputies ate here every day, and any smart criminal would have scoped the place out in advance to save both himself and everyone else grief.

Of course, desperate people did desperate things, and this man seemed very near the brink. Eric took in the scene and tried to decide how best to handle the situation.

Cat Murphy, the petite, no-nonsense owner of Cat's Courthouse Café, stood just to the left of the man holding waitress Julia Daniels near a wall that gave the culprit a bird's-eye view of both the entrance door and the kitchen. Cat's expression showed shock, but her eyes held a kind of resolve that didn't bode well for the grungy-looking man who'd disrupted the last minutes of the lunch hour. Cat had been married to a police officer who was killed in the line of duty. And given that Julia Daniels was related to Cat and had moved here about five months ago at Cat's request, Cat sure wasn't going to stand by and let anything bad happen to her. That made her not only dangerous but impulsive, too, Eric reasoned.

But right now he was more worried about Julia. He liked her a lot, had even thought about asking her out on a date. So that made him just a tad dangerous, too. Not impulsive like motherly Cat, yet dangerous just the same. But he had to protect Julia and everybody else in here, somehow. *Help me, Lord.*

The other diners had stopped eating to stare with fright at the man and woman in the corner of the room. And Eric's buddy and fellow deputy Adam Dupont was sitting across from Eric, his trigger finger itching from the way the pulse was pounding in his jawline.

"Steady," Eric whispered to Adam. "He looks real serious about using that gun."

"Shut up!" The robber's fidgety, shifting gaze moved from Eric to Adam. "I mean it, *man*. You two need to take out your guns and slide them across the floor."

Eric glanced at his friend, sending Adam a silent message. Then he nodded. Best not to argue with the man holding the gun to the blonde's head. Besides, she looked as pale as a ghost, her big gold-green eyes widening each time the gun was pressed harder against her temple.

Carefully, with one hand in the air, both deputies took out their weapons. "Okay," Eric said. "I'm gonna send them both your way."

The robber nodded, then waited, watching intently as Eric did as he'd promised. The only sound in the tiny café was that of weapons hitting linoleum and fat hitting the grill as the guns flew across the black-and-white-patterned floor.

"What do you want?" Julia managed to ask the man, her tone shaky.

The man holding Julia glanced around, hesitant at first, sweat popping out on his forehead. He eyed the back of Julia's head so close to his own, then glanced around the restaurant as if he were looking for something or someone. Then his gaze skittered to the counter near the kitchen.

"I need some cash," the burly man replied, lifting his chin toward the back of the restaurant. "All of it."

Cat nodded. "I'll have to go behind the cash register. Don't hurt Julia, okay. You can have the money, but you don't need to hurt anyone."

"Shut up and get it." Then he pressed the gun closer to Julia's tousled hair a little harder. "And let me worry about *Julia*."

The robber shifted around, facing Cat as she slowly moved toward the counter in the far corner of the room, forcing Julia to turn. "And if anybody tries anything, I'll kill her."

Eric watched as Julia pivoted around with the man, her willowy frame shaking, her shoulder-length golden hair swishing over her black-and-white uniform. The woman was terrified, but she was cooperating. That showed she had common sense at least. He just prayed she wouldn't try anything crazy, like fighting this man. He stared at her, willing her to let Adam and him do their jobs.

Her gaze met Eric's and held. She seemed to be silently screaming a message at him. He could see the plea in her eyes, could almost feel exactly what she was thinking: What about my little girl? What will happen to her if I die?

He knew from hearing Julia and Cat chattering away as they worked that Julia was Cat's cousin and she was a widow with an eight-year-old daughter named Moria. And he also knew that she was a devoted mother. He'd seen both mother and child in church last Sunday.

He wanted to see both of them there again next Sunday, too. So he held her gaze, hoping he could relay a sense of calm to her. He sat silently, his mind screaming for her to hold on. I won't let anything happen to you, I promise. He inclined his head just an inch, but it seemed to be enough to give her courage. She lifted her chin a notch in response.

Eric tore his gaze away, then tilted his head toward Adam. They'd worked together for the past seven years, to the point where they could almost read each other's minds. He hoped Adam was doing that very thing right now. They needed a distraction.

But they also needed to be very, very careful so no one in here would end up dead.

Especially the pretty blonde who'd only lived in Wildflower for a few months. Julia might be new to the area and new to the café, but she was already a favorite among the lunch crowd.

Eric liked Julia, even though he didn't know that much about her. He surely wasn't going to sit by and witness something horrible happening to a hardworking, quiet, pretty woman who didn't bother anyone. No, sir. That wasn't gonna happen. Not today, at least. And not before he'd had some of Cat's famous hamburger steak and mashed potatoes.

Be still and know that I am God. That verse played through Julia's head, so she stood still and decided to keep her eyes on the deputy sheriff. There was something about Eric Butler that made her feel safe. Maybe it was his quiet, controlled nature, or the way he tried to put everyone he encountered at ease. He had always been polite to Julia, in spite of his friend Adam's jokes and flirtatious nature. Eric didn't flirt. He just made small talk and asked her about Moria, his chocolate-colored eyes full of life and contentment. Eric had a secure, sure masculine presence that could fill a room. That presence, that security, such a contrast to her late husband's passive personality, was the only thing keeping Julia sane right now. She said a prayer, silently and quickly. *Please, God, help us.* She hadn't turned to God very much throughout the ordeal of her husband's death. But she sure needed Him here today. Because of Moria.

Julia kept telling herself to stay calm, to do as the skittish robber holding her body in front of his as a shield had said, to not move. But it wasn't so easy. She was worried about Moria. Her daughter was safe at school. She had to keep repeating that phrase inside her head, her heart pounding in cadence with the rapid breaths of the man holding her. Moria was safe; she had to be. Isn't that why she'd taken Cat's advice and left

San Antonio to come to this nice, quiet little town all the way across Texas, near the Louisiana border? *Moria is safe. Please, Lord, keep her safe.*

Safe. Julia had brought her daughter here after her husband Alfonso had been murdered while he was working late one night. Murdered at his fancy desk in the high-rise De La Noche building in downtown San Antonio. And Moria had been there with him, hidden in the ladies' lounge down the hall, dialing Julia's number on her father's cell phone even as the murder had taken place, from what the authorities could piece together.

"Tell Mommy to come right now," Moria had repeated to Julia and the police after they'd found her sitting in a chair in the lounge, her doll Rosa clutched in one hand and the phone in the other. "Daddy said we were playing a game, like hide-and-seek. He said to talk to you and tell you to come and find me. Where's my daddy?"

Julia hadn't been able right then to tell the little girl that her daddy was dead. That had taken all of Julia's courage a few hours later at home.

Julia and the therapists still weren't sure what Moria had seen or heard that night. The little girl didn't talk about it much and the therapists couldn't agree on the validity of repressed memories. But her nightmares told the tale of horror Moria had gone through, sitting there all alone, waiting for her parents that night at the De La Noche complex.

Alfonso had worked for the Gardonez family since high school, only to end up dead.

Of the night. The La Flor De La Noche, or the flower of the night, was what had started the Gardonez family dynasty over one hundred years ago in Mexico. Night-blooming jasmine, moonflowers and the beautiful but deadly angel trumpet, started from seeds, and one woman's determination, had created a legend within the floral industry. Now the Gardonez family not only grew beautiful flowers but also farmed and marketed vegetables and fruit, too. And they had worldwide distribution, with a trucking and shipping company that was the industry standard.

But someone within their ranks, or someone who wanted to do the company harm, apparently had a secret that had killed her husband. Did her child also know that secret?

Now, as Julia stood here in the bruising grip of an armed man, she had to wonder if that secret had followed her all the way across Texas. She didn't know anything for sure; she only wanted to protect her daughter. But she did know that something had been bothering Alfonso before his death. Something that had him up at night and brooding all day long. Something that had told Julia not to let him pick up Moria from school that day. It was as if he'd also known something bad might happen to him. As if he'd known he'd have to take some sort of secret to his grave.

What if this man wanted that secret? What if this man hadn't come here just to rob the café? What if he'd come for her, instead?

Eric sensed the war behind those pretty golden-green eyes. He knew that look. Julia was weighing her options. He'd seen that kind of confused, centered gaze before in the eyes of men who'd made the wrong choices and regretted them. He'd also seen it in the eyes of other victims, haunted and frightened, wondering and waiting. She was afraid, but she held her head up with a determination that caused him to admire her. The woman had so much to live for. She had a child. He only hoped that spark of spunk shining inside her eyes wouldn't get her killed.

And he hoped this nagging feeling inside his gut would just go away, that it wasn't a sign of things to come. He didn't like this at all. The man had come in through the door and zoomed right in on Julia instead of the cash register. Now, why was that? Eric wondered.

"What now?" Adam asked as he watched Cat fumbling with the cash register.

"We wait," Eric replied under his breath.

Cat started walking slowly back toward Julia and the man, her ever-present red cowboy boots clicking against the linoleum, her eyes slanting toward Eric and Adam. She knew they would stop this. She had to know. Cat trusted them, as did everyone else in this sleepy little town. Eric gave Cat a reassuring look, holding his breath as she neared the gunman.

The robber clutched at Julia and said the words no lawman ever wanted to hear. "I'm gonna have to take *her* with me. Just until I get down the road." He pushed at Julia. "Hold the money."

Adam shot Eric a look. The chances of Julia surviving this once the strung-out man took her to another location were slim to none. There was no apparent reason for this man to take a hostage. Well, except maybe that he knew the two deputy sheriffs staring him down would surely come after him. They had to do something before the culprit got Julia away from the premises, or this could go from bad to worse.

Cat shook her head, obviously thinking the same thing, her usually down-to-earth candor breaking. "You've got the money. Please let her go."

But the man wasn't listening. He kept pushing at Julia. "Take it, so we can get out of here!"

And then everything happened at once.

One minute Cat was stretching her hand out, pressing a wad of cash toward Julia, her gaze meeting Julia's in a silent communication. Then Cat went into action, and instead of handing Julia the money, she dropped it just out of Julia's reach, all around the robber's feet. Adam took over, scraping his chair back with just enough abrasiveness to cause the robber to tear his eyes away from the fluttering money falling to the floor. The robber turned, yanking Julia around as Adam skidded his chair again, this time knocking it over and slamming his body behind it for protection.

Eric yelled, "Get down! Everyone get down!"

The frantic robber shook his gun in the air, giving Julia a split second to kick Eric's gun back toward him. Watching the gun slide across the floor, the robber grabbed at Julia, holding her tightly as he spun around to shoot at Adam and Eric. Adam ducked low, while Eric slid his body across the floor in a drop and roll, diving for the gun Julia had sent his way. It landed right on his trigger finger.

Julia watched in horror as the two deputies went into action. Then Cat's hand dug into her arm, pulling her free as the man waved his gun and dived for the fallen money all around his feet.

And then Julia heard the deputy scream again, "Get down! Everybody down!"

Julia saw Deputy Butler lift his gun and skid back toward the protection of his table at the same time the robber aimed his own gun toward the deputy.

Julia waited, her breath held, for the man to fire. Instead, he pushed Cat away and grabbed Julia again. "She's going with me. Get it?" He had the gun back at her head, but he was shaking almost as hard as Julia. Maybe because Deputy Butler now had his own weapon aimed at the robber.

Julia looked at Eric, saw the message clear in his eyes. He wasn't going to let this madman take her.

"Over my dead body," the deputy said, his determined eyes centered on the criminal holding Julia. "Now do us all a favor and drop the weapon."

Julia looked from Eric to Cat, wondering what she could do to get away. Then she remembered the swinging door. If she twisted ever so slightly, she could use it as leverage to make the man lose his balance. Mustering all her strength, she fought against the man holding her, twisting until she could see the door in her peripheral vision. Hearing her own scream locked inside her head, or maybe she was screaming out loud, she braced herself as the robber held her tight, dragging her toward the kitchen door. "I have to take her, man. I have to. I don't want to hurt anyone, but I have to take her with me." He held the gun close. Guiding Julia backward with him, he reached the swinging door, then stood inches away.

"Don't do it," Adam called, standing up. "Just drop the gun and we'll get you some help."

The man shook his head. "Can't do that." Then in one swift motion, he grunted, tugging Julia toward the rickety old door. Julia took one last look at Eric Butler, hoping to give him a sign that she wasn't going to go willingly through that door.

But Eric was watching the man holding her. "Don't make me shoot you. Because I can bring you down before you ever pull that trigger."

"Try it," the robber goaded, stepping back, the swinging door now inches behind him.

Julia knew if they got past the swinging door, she might not live to see her daughter again. She had to do something right now. With a grunt and all the force she could muster she pushed with one foot against the wobbly door, then grabbed the solid wood frame with both hands as she used her body to slam against the man behind her. When she felt him shifting backward, she held on to the frame so she wouldn't fall with him, steeling herself against the chance of getting shot.

Shocked to find himself moving through the open space, the man had no choice but to loosen his grip on Julia and grab for a handhold. While Julia lunged back against the robber, Cat pushed at the door, causing the confused man to let go of Julia as he went falling through the open doorway. He hollered his displeasure, then lifted his gun in the air as he lost his balance. A round of shots rang out. Then the man grunted as he went flying into the kitchen. Scrambling up, he clutched his left arm, then ran out the back door of the kitchen, leaving Julia crumpled on her knees, shaking, as she clung to the door frame. The swish of the door banging back toward Julia's slumping body echoed through the building, followed by the slamming of the metal back door. The man was gone and she was still alive.

And then silence, followed by a rush of action all around her.

"It's over, honey," Cat said, pulling Julia up to hug her close. "It's all over."

Adam jumped up, heading for the kitchen door. "I think you hit him, Eric. Everybody okay?"

People begin lifting off the floor. Julia heard women crying and saw a crowd gathered at the front door. A buzz of energy surrounded the screams still echoing inside her head. Her ears were ringing; her blood pressure was pumping inside her temple. But she was alive.

Thanks to Deputy Butler. He'd shot the man holding her. She knew, because she had splatters of blood on her white shirt.

"Where's the other deputy?" she asked Cat as Adam brushed past her, her head coming up to search for Eric.

And then she saw him, lying behind an upturned table with blood covering his left shoulder. He wasn't moving.

"He needs help!" Julia shouted, pointing toward Eric. "Somebody help him."

"Eric?" Adam bolted around, then screamed, "Call 911, Cat. Eric's been shot." He headed past Julia and through the kitchen door, already talking into his radio about being in pursuit. "I'm going after him!"

The call was unnecessary. Julia could hear the sirens and the banging of the front door as the café became swamped with deputies and policemen and the lone reporter from the town newspaper, the *Wildflower Gazette*.

The first responders looked over the place and took

in the grim scenario, then started moving people out of the café, which had now become a crime scene.

"He saved my life." Julia went limp against the wall, all of the strength drained out of her as the reporter's camera flashed in her face. Deputy Butler had saved her life.

And now he might be dead because of it.

TWO

Eric woke up in the emergency room, his left shoulder throbbing to beat the band.

Trying to raise his head, he called out, "What—"

A gray-haired nurse pushed him back down. "Easy, cowboy. You've been shot and you're about to go into surgery to debride the wound. We just need to clean it out a little bit, make sure everything's intact in there. You're lucky, though. Bullet went straight through without hitting any major arteries or bones."

"Bullet?" Eric lay back, trying to remember. Then it all came rushing back. Julia Daniels. An armed robbery. The man was going to take Julia as a hostage. They'd exchanged gunfire. Darkness and voices in his head. Adam telling him to hang on. Now he had vague flashes of the EMS team…someone applying pressure to his wound, asking him questions about his medical history, a needle shoved into his arm.

"The waitress?" he managed to croak over the sound

of doctors rushing all around, poking him here and there and shouting out orders about X-rays and vital signs.

"That pretty little thing," the nurse said as she checked the IV drip, her expression all business. "She's just fine. Outside waiting with your family to hear how you're doing, though. She said you saved her life."

Eric managed a weak grin. "My buddy Adam did most of the hard work."

"Yeah, right. But you shot the bad guy."

Eric tried to lift up again. His bloody shirt was gone. "The robber, where…is he?"

The nurse shook her head. "From what we're hearing, he got clean away. But don't fret, now. Your buddies have put out an APB on him."

Eric tried to speak, but his fatigue, coupled with whatever medication they were pumping into him, caused drowsiness to overtake him. He went to sleep with the memory of Julia's face, front and center in his frazzled mind.

Julia paced the tiny E.R. sitting room, her sturdy, black wedge-heeled work shoes clumping with each step. Cat had insisted she go home and rest, but Julia was too keyed up to do that. After rushing to the elementary school to check on Moria—no, make that after making a scene at the school because she was so frantic to make sure her daughter was safe—and then checking Moria out and taking her to the neighbor's house just to be sure, she'd come straight here. And she planned on being right here when Eric Butler came out of surgery.

Thank goodness Mrs. Ulmer hadn't minded watching Moria. Julia knew Moria would be safe with the Ulmers. They'd seen how upset she'd been and promised to keep Moria inside and quiet. Even though he didn't get out much these days, Mr. Ulmer had once been an avid hunter and he'd assured her he'd watch over Moria, using one of his many rifles and shotguns if need be. But there had been enough shooting for one day, Julia thought, her mind reliving how the gunman had tried to take her and how Eric had fired a shot to stop him. Then she remembered seeing Eric lying there, bleeding and unmoving.

Please don't let him die, she prayed.

She'd seen too much death lately.

And her daughter had seen enough grief and death to last her a lifetime.

That thought caused Julia's knees to go weak. Sinking down in a fabric-covered blue chair, she put her head in her hands and prayed that Moria didn't hear about this. She'd warned the Ulmers not to discuss it in front of her already-fragile daughter.

"You okay?"

Julia looked up to find Adam and Cat standing in front of her. Cat settled in the chair beside her while Adam stood with his hands in his pants pockets, looking as worried about his friend as she felt.

Down the way in another chair, Eric's father, Harlan, sat staring at the tiled floor. Julia had introduced herself to him the minute she'd come in the door, telling him how much she appreciated what Eric had done for her. But Mr. Butler had only grunted and nodded, his eyes so like his son's, blank and unyielding, in spite of their warmth.

Harlan Butler was a retired sheriff's deputy himself, who, according to Cat, now lived out on the lake in a cabin his son had apparently built right next to his own house. Eric wanted his widowed father near, which only endeared him to Julia since she'd never been close with her own parents. So now the Butler men lived on connecting lots, two bachelors enjoying their time as father and son. Mr. Butler certainly understood the risks of the job. But right now that didn't help matters. Right now they were all worried, and somehow Julia couldn't help but feel responsible for all of this.

"I'm fine," Julia said in answer to Cat's question, shaking her head as she stared at the lone man at the other end of the hall. "I couldn't go home. I had to come and see—"

"If he's gonna be all right," Cat finished, her arm going around Julia's shoulder. "We're all right here, honey, praying for him. I think the whole town is praying right now. That was mighty close." She glanced at Harlan, too. "His daddy is real worried, I can tell you." Then she lowered her voice. "Of course, a Texas lawman can't show his true emotions. It's an unwritten code." She shot Adam a pointed look. "Got to be tough as nails, every last one of 'em."

Julia closed her eyes, reliving the vivid scene trapped inside her mind. She wasn't as tough as nails. She could still feel the cold steel of that gun pressing at her temple. And she wondered for the hundredth time if that bright, stark terror was how her husband Alfonso had felt just before he died.

Was that the kind of terror her daughter experienced each time she suffered another horrible nightmare about her father?

Alfonso. She remembered sitting in another hospital room, waiting to hear the details of her husband's brutal death.

She didn't want to hear that again today. She didn't want that nice, unassuming sheriff's deputy to die. Not on her account. Not for something as stupid as a robbery that would have yielded very little money.

Trying to make sense of everything, she looked up at Adam. "Did you find the robber?"

Adam shook his head. "No. He took off like lightning. Pretty sure there was a getaway car parked around the corner, and in all the confusion we missed it." He looked as if he were taking that failure very personally. "He was bleeding, so he's wounded. I tried to find him, searched behind the restaurant and all the streets, too. Sent a patrol out. He either found a good hiding spot, or someone came back just in time to get him in a car. Found some blood, but that's about it." Then he lowered his head, unable to look at Julia. "Of course, we have the bloodstains from your blouse, too."

Julia looked down at the clean lightweight sweater Cat had offered her after the police had asked her to remove her uniform blouse. Wishing she could go home and take a long shower to wash away all the fear and doubt, she could only nod toward Adam. "When will you know something?"

"Not sure," Adam said. "It'll take the state crime lab a while to get to it, but we've put a rush on it."

Then he rolled his head, trying to release some of the obvious tension coiling through his muscles. "We've put out an all-points bulletin, and we're checking all the area hospitals for any incoming bullet wounds. We've got roadblocks set up all around the area, too. I'm hoping they'll haul him in any minute now, and I want to be the first person to get at him, trust me." He shook his head, then pounded his fist against the wall. "I let him slip right through my fingers."

Cat gave him a soft smile. "Don't be so hard on yourself. You and Eric did the best you could today. It was crazy, there, after he ran out. Nobody blames you. You and Eric saved Julia from becoming a hostage."

Adam looked at the floor. "There's a lot about this that just doesn't make sense. But we'll get the details figured out. We're running a search right now, based on the descriptions we got from other witnesses. The boys will call when they have something conclusive on both him and the weapon. We found the bullet lodged in the front door."

Cat asked, "And Eric?"

"He kept going in and out of consciousness, telling me he was okay, that it didn't hurt too much. Of course that was right before he passed out cold." Hearing Julia's low groan, he said, "Don't worry. He's been through worse playing football back in high school."

Then he glanced over at Cat, causing Julia to wonder if they were keeping something from her. Eric and Cat were close. Just how close Julia couldn't be sure, but she knew they shared a lot with each other.

Feeling left out and afraid, Julia looked at her older cousin. "Cat, is everything okay back at the restaurant?"

"I had to shut her down, of course, so the investigators could look for evidence," Cat said with a shrug, her dark curls shimmering around her face. "Who wants to eat there today, or ever again, for that matter?"

"Ah, now, you can't quit," Adam said, his grin tight with tension. "Who'd keep me fed and watered?"

"You sound like an old mule," Cat retorted, her own smile weak. "I'm not gonna shut down forever. Just… needed to get away from there. The employees are still a tad jumpy."

"We're all jumpy," Adam replied. "And right now

your place is a crime scene, so we had to close the doors, anyway. Technically, I'm on administrative duty only until the Rangers get through investigating." Then he looked down the hall at Harlan. "Hey, why don't I go find us some coffee? I'll ask Harlan if he wants some, too. Won't be as good as yours, of course, Cat, but it might help."

"Yeah, coffee," Cat said. "Just what we need to calm the jitters."

"I'm just offering," he said with a shrug.

"Go on," Cat said, her smile full of understanding. "I'll take mine black. Julia?"

"Nothing for me," Julia said, an uneasy feeling setting her stomach on yet another spasm of jangled, tingling nerves. "I just wish I knew who that man was."

"I'll call and harass the investigators," Adam said. "We all want to know that."

After he'd left, Cat turned to Julia, her big brown eyes full of concern. "So how's Moria?"

Julia looked at her watch. "She's fine. Mrs. Ulmer probably doesn't like me calling every five minutes, though." She was torn between staying here or just rushing to the Ulmers' to get her daughter.

"Adam put a man on her, you know."

Julia's head came up, her heart racing. "Why? Is there something else—?"

"No, honey," Cat said, her hand covering Julia's. "Eric asked him to do it, in one of his more lucid moments just before they put him in the ambulance. Told Adam to send someone to check on your little girl."

"How'd he know?" Julia said, amazed. "How'd he know to do that?" Or that the gesture would set her mind at ease. "You didn't tell him anything, did you?"

Cat chuckled, soft and low. "No, against my better judgment, and because I promised you I wouldn't, I haven't told anyone about your troubles." Then she looked down the hall toward the operating rooms. "But Eric can see things—that's why he's such a good lawman. The man has a sensitive side he hides from the world. He probably figured a mother would be concerned about the safety of her child—I mean after being held at gunpoint. And with the robber still on the loose."

Julia nodded, rubbed her suddenly cold hands together. "I *was* worried. The school's principal couldn't understand why I wanted to pull her out of class, since they have a sheriff's deputy as their resource officer, but I'm glad I did. I'll call Mrs. Ulmer again in a few minutes, but I'm sure Mr. Ulmer will entertain her all afternoon."

"You can count on that," Cat replied. "The Ulmers love Moria like their own grandchildren. She sure is a sweetheart." Then she let out a sigh. "Boy, I'm beat. What a day."

Julia looked at her cousin, grateful for Cat's calming presence. They'd always been close growing up, so when Cat offered Julia a job and a place to live to get her away from San Antonio and all the bad memories, Julia had jumped at the chance to start over in Wildflower. Although Cat was a few years older than Julia's thirty-two, with her stylish curly bob and her big dark eyes, she looked younger than her actual age. Petite and becomingly plump, Cat was one of the nicest people Julia had ever met, a true Texan through and through. Cat loved God, people and her job. She loved to cook, especially for all the deputies and police officers who frequented her establishment. Maybe because her own husband had been a lawman and had died doing his job about five years ago.

Working at the café was like having one big, law-abiding family, Julia thought. Cat kept telling her she'd be safe in Wildflower. And living in this quiet town near Caddo Lake did make her feel safe.

That was something she'd never had before.

Thinking this whole thing had probably brought Cat some awful flashbacks, too, Julia leaned close. "Are *you* okay?"

Cat brushed at her hair with one hand. "Me? Yeah, sure. I guess I'm used to all the commotion. I tell you, though, when that man was holding that gun to your head, I 'bout had a heart attack. We just don't get that kind of crime here."

"Eric and Adam saved my life. They saved all of us," Julia said, not sure how to comfort Cat. They'd both lost their husbands, but Cat's man had been a true-blue Texas Ranger. Alfonso Endicott, on the other hand, had been a "yes" man. A hardworking man, but a man always willing to do the bidding of his powerful bosses, nonetheless. She shouldn't hold that against him, but there it was, bitter and heavy, inside her.

Alfonso had sacrificed being with his wife and child to stay at the beck and call of the Gardonez family. And all for the love of money. Alfonso always wanted more, needed more, to prove himself. He'd gone beyond the call of duty in order to keep his high-paying job. The Gardonez family had depended on him to take care of their millions, to make sure everything they did was above board and by the books.

Then why had someone killed him?

Julia had a funny feeling that the motive had to do with money, too, since her husband had been the head accountant for the De La Noche Shipping Company. That brought her thoughts back to today's events.

"Why did that man try to rob us right in the middle of lunch hour, Cat?" she asked, hoping her cousin could put a reasonable spin on things, because Julia didn't want to put her own spin on it. She wasn't ready to delve into all the implications right now.

Cat gave her an eloquent shrug. "I guess he needed some cash. Maybe for drugs, or maybe he just took a wrong turn somewhere. Or maybe he was being stupid. We've never been robbed before, ever, and I've been running the café for over a decade, and my mama before me for even longer than that herself. You've spent enough summers here with me growing up to know that. It's just plain weird."

Julia had to agree. She'd often traveled here with her parents to visit Cat's family. They'd leave her in Wild-flower for weeks on end while they traveled around in their RV camper. Julia had loved staying with her aunt and uncle and Cat and helping out at the café. And even though she just had Cat now, she liked working at the café and living right around the corner from her cousin. Or she had up until today.

"I hope we find out something soon about Eric. And that other man, too."

Cat nodded. "Well, just think…you and Eric will both be famous from now on. Adam, too, probably. Even the restaurant, for that matter."

Julia pushed a hand through her hair. "How's that?"

"The *Gazette,* honey. Mickey Jameson is doing a front-page spread about the robbery. He wanted to interview you, but I held him back. Told him to give you a call later today before the paper goes to press." Seeing the look on Julia's face, she put a hand to her mouth. "Oh, my. I wasn't even thinking straight—"

Julia jumped out of her chair. "Front page? I don't want to be on the front page."

But it was too late. The double doors leading from the E.R. driveway swished open and in walked debonair Mickey Jameson himself. "Ah, there's my star witness," he said, smiling broadly. "Got a great shot of you, Mrs. Daniels. Now I just need to finish the story. Cat, I know you said to wait, but I have a deadline. And you know what they say—'If it bleeds, it leads.'"

Julia shook her head, backing away. "I'm not going to talk to you, Mr. Jameson. Not now, not ever."

Eric woke up in the recovery room, his wounded shoulder bandaged but still throbbing. At least now his head wasn't nearly as fuzzy. Finally he could take his time and remember everything that had happened during the robbery.

Lying back, he tried to think things through, but something just wasn't right about the situation. Before he could figure it all out, his father walked in.

"You awake?"

Eric looked toward the end of the bed where his broad-shouldered father stood with his hands in the pockets of his jeans. "I'm fine, Dad. How'd you get in here, anyway?"

"I still have some connections. Managed to sweet-talk a nurse."

Eric grinned at that. "Some things never change."

Harlan didn't dwell on hospital procedure. "Bullet skipped right through you, did it?"

"Yep. I don't know why they even brought me to the hospital. I could have gone home and poured some alcohol on it and been good as new." In spite of the jovial tone, Eric could see the worry in his father's eyes. "Bullet went straight in and out, Pop. Probably still stuck somewhere in the café wall."

Harlan kicked one boot against the other, as if he had mud on his shoes. "Good. That's evidence now."

"Yep. I'm sure they'll find the bullet. I just wish I knew why that guy chose lunchtime to go and rob the place."

"Yep, that is kinda odd. Most wait until closing time." He stood silent for a couple of beats, then added, "Mighty strange how he got clear out of town so fast, too."

"I'm gonna figure it out," Eric said. "I shot the man, but I need answers."

"Just be careful," Harlan replied, rocking back on his worn cowboy boots. "You'll need to rest up for a few days at least."

"I'll be on leave until the department finishes its investigation. Did they call in the Rangers?"

Harlan nodded. "Standard procedure. But you could use a rest, anyway. You've been burning the candle at both ends for a while, now."

"I guess I have at that," Eric replied, tiredness sweeping over him. And today, of all days, he'd planned on having a nice, leisurely lunch with his friend just so he could enjoy watching Julia Daniels go about her work. No rest for the weary. "You okay?"

"I'm good," Harlan said, clearing his throat. "Just waiting for them to put you in a room. Then I'll go on home and check on the animals."

"You don't have to come back tonight. I'll probably sleep the night through, then be home tomorrow."

Harlan nodded, his white-haired head down. "That waitress came and sat with me for a while during your surgery. She's mighty grateful."

"Julia? She's a nice woman."

"Do you know much about her?" Harlan put both hands on the steel footboard of the bed. "I mean, it struck me how she didn't want Mickey to put her picture in the paper, didn't even want to talk to him about the robbery and all. Either she's real shy, or she really doesn't want any publicity. Mighty odd to me."

Eric moved his head, his eyes locking with his daddy's. They were both probably wondering the same things. Instincts and natural curiosity made both of them good lawmen.

"No, I don't know a whole lot about Julia Daniels, except that she's related to Cat," Eric replied. "But I aim to find out everything I can." For more reasons than he wanted to explain to his clever father.

He'd been very aware of Julia since she'd started working at the café, mainly because she was pretty and pleasant and, well, he was single and lonely. But now that awareness had changed into concern and suspicion. Eric couldn't answer why, except that today's event had certainly put Julia in the spotlight. And like that nosy Mickey Jameson, Eric had some questions of his own. He didn't want a story for the front page, though. He wanted the truth, especially since it occurred to him that even the usually talkative Cat hadn't given up much information about her pretty cousin.

"I think that's wise," Harlan said, satisfied they'd cleared up that little matter of concern. "Might need to know what all we're dealing with here."

Eric lay back against his pillows, watching as his father threw up his hand and headed out the door.

"You can count on that," he said to himself.

THREE

"C'mon, honey. Time for bed."

Julia tugged on Moria's hand, the sweet soapy smell surrounding her daughter causing her heart to swell with love. Glancing out the window where the streetlight illuminated the whole backyard and Cat's big rambling white Victorian house just beyond, she wondered for the hundredth time today if they were truly safe here.

She *should* feel safe, since Deputy Sheriff Adam Dupont had come by not an hour ago to check on them, and to give her a report on Eric. They would only allow his father in to see him after his surgery. Adam had assured her Eric would be home in a day or so.

He'd also assured her that Eric didn't want her to feel bad about things. It wasn't her fault, Adam kept saying. Eric wouldn't want her to worry at all. He'd be up and about in no time. But not back on the job just yet. His injury and an internal investigation of the shooting would see to that.

"Eric will get in some fishing, at least, while he's on leave," Adam had quipped. "He can toss a line and catch fish with just one hand, easy."

"Easy," Julia said now as she tried to put her uneasiness out of her mind. She focused instead on getting her daughter to bed.

Moria, dressed in a frilly pink nightgown and clutching her favorite doll, stood just inside her bedroom door, her big dark eyes surveying the dainty, feminine room. "I'm not sleepy, Mommy."

Julia prayed this wouldn't turn into another stand-off. True, it had become increasingly easier to get Moria to bed since they'd moved here, but every now and then Moria still had a bad night. The rental house that had been originally built for Cat's late grandmother was purposely small, with just a den/kitchen combination across the front, a short hallway with a bath and laundry room to one side and two bedrooms on the other side. There was a clear view of both the well-lit front and back yards. No hidden nooks and crannies, no big deep closets or long winding stairways like those in the house back in San Antonio. She'd sold that gaudy dwelling for way under the appraisal value just to have moving money and a small nest egg to go with Alfonso's life insurance, most of which she'd tucked away for her daughter's future.

Small and safe, Julia reminded herself, glancing around at the clutter-free house. Simple and uncomplicated. Secure. No hiding places. Back at the big house, Moria had loved to play hide-and-seek with her daddy. But here, Julia discouraged that particular game.

Now Julia prayed they weren't about to enter another kind of hide-and-seek. But the man who'd held her at gunpoint was still out there somewhere, she reminded herself. How could he have just disappeared in broad daylight? And where was he now?

"Moria, it's past your bedtime," she said, looking back over her shoulder to make sure the solid front door was dead-bolted. "You've had a big day, so I know you're tired."

"But tomorrow's Saturday," Moria pointed out, jumping up onto the ruffled yellow-rose-patterned spread covering her twin four-poster bed. Pushing stuffed animals, fashion dolls, and fluffy pillows aside, she added, "Rosa and I aren't tired, honestly, Mommy." She squeezed her favorite doll.

Julia shook her head then laughed. "Mr. Ulmer told me how you and he raced around the backyard today. He said you won every race."

"But I was on my bike," Moria said, her hands wrapped against her midsection. "Mr. Ulmer lets me ride the bike he bought for his grandchildren while he rides his scooter. Rosa sat in the basket."

"That's awfully nice of him," Julia said, silently thanking God for the Ulmers. The couple lived right next door and had immediately taken a shine to Moria.

Once they'd heard Julia needed after-school care for those days she worked late at the café, they'd volunteered, no questions asked, even though Mr. Ulmer had horribly arthritic knees and had to get around with a motorized scooter most days. And they didn't even want any pay. But Julia made sure she did other things for them to compensate, such as bringing home leftovers from the café, or picking up extra groceries whenever she was going to the store. Today, especially, they had managed to distract Moria while the awful details of the shooting had blared across the local news stations.

Including her face and her name, Julia thought, unease causing her next words to come out harshly. "Moria, no more excuses. It's bedtime. You might not be tired, but *I* sure am."

Remembering her brief discussion at the hospital today with the overbearing *Gazette* reporter, Julia let out a sigh. She only hoped the paper wouldn't make too much of this. She wanted to stay low-key. But Mickey Jameson kept pushing, telling her this was big news and readers would want to hear her side of the story. After all, she'd been in the clutches of an armed robber and she'd survived, due to the two deputy sheriffs who'd risked their own lives to save her.

How could she refuse such a request without looking ungrateful, Julia thought. So she'd given him a brief description of how the robbery had taken place, but she'd been very careful not to reveal too much personal information. Besides, her hair was longer now, and she didn't wear the fancy clothes or the expensive cosmetics she'd favored while living in San Antonio. Most days, she hardly recognized herself in the mirror. So maybe no one else would, either. And after Alfonso had died, she'd had her name legally changed back to her maiden name, just as an added precaution. Maybe she'd covered all her bases. She prayed she had, for Moria's sake at least.

"Want to lie on my bed and rest?" Moria asked, her brown eyes going wide as she brought Julia out of her troubled thoughts. "Rosa and I can make room."

Julia grinned, then touched a hand to her daughter's dark curls, seeing the hopeful look in her eyes. "How about I read you a bedtime story?" Julia offered, hoping to distract both of them for a few minutes. "That way I can rest my feet and you can get sleepy."

Moria bobbed her head. "Can I pick?"

"Of course," Julia said, watching as her daughter ran to the small bookcase beneath the window. "But not too long, okay?"

Moria giggled, then found a suitable book. "Rosa likes this one."

Julia nodded, then snuggled up with her daughter, the ever-present doll Moria had named Rosa cuddled between them, her flower-strewn lacy yellow dress and her rose-encased little drawstring purse perfectly displayed.

Alfonso had given Moria the doll for her birthday last year because her dress had matched Moria's yellow rose-decorated bedroom back in San Antonio and because the doll had reminded him of Moria. That had been a few days before his death. Which was probably why Moria clung to the doll from the minute she arrived home from school each day until she fell asleep at night.

Even after they'd moved here, Moria had begged for the same colors in this bedroom. Julia had readily agreed, hoping to make her daughter feel at home. The room looked like a rose garden, complete with a dainty silk oversize yellow rose sitting in a clay pot on the dresser. The rose looked so real, Julia reached out and touched it. Alfonso had loved yellow roses.

Looking down at the doll's beautiful porcelain face and jet-black hair with its miniature combs and curls, Julia once again thought about Alfonso. He'd loved Moria so much. He would have never intentionally put his child in danger. And yet the night he'd been murdered Moria had been in danger. She'd been in the office with her father, hidden away.

I should have picked her up that day, Julia thought.

But she'd been running late from attending a charity event all afternoon, and Alfonso had been insistent. He wanted to spend time with their daughter, but in doing so, he'd inadvertently brought danger to all of them. At least he'd had the foresight to get Moria out of harm's way once he'd seen that danger coming. He'd given her his phone and dialed up Julia, leaving Moria alone but safe. He'd known Julia was at a nearby hotel finishing up with her duties after the charity event.

Now Moria's secrets about what she'd seen or heard that night were also hidden away, deeply embedded inside her child's mind because no one, not the team of therapists or her own mother, could bring it all to the surface for Moria. She kept whatever she knew intact. That is, until she went to sleep at night.

Then, all the horrible scary things hidden in the dark seemed to come out to taunt the little girl.

No wonder her daughter never wanted to go to sleep.

And no wonder Julia was so worried that the secrets locked inside her daughter's mind might bring harm to both of them. Not knowing was driving her crazy.

But finding out the truth might be even more danger-ous.

He had to know the truth.

Eric stared at the yellow crime-scene tape slashing across the double doors of Cat's Courthouse Café. He'd come here straight from the hospital, and although his arm was in a sling and he still felt woozy from all the pain medication, it felt good to be out in the bright springtime day with a fresh breeze blowing over his face. His shoulder still ached, but his mind was spinning like the whimsical metallic garden ornament Cat had hanging by the front door. He stood back, leaning against the old-fashioned hitching rail in front of the café, his mind reliving every minute of what had happened here two days ago.

"Got it figured out yet, buddy?" Adam asked as he came up and handed Eric a bottle of soda. "Thought you could use a drink."

"Thanks," Eric said, taking a long swig of the amber liquid. Then he glanced back through the windows of the restaurant. "He went in through the kitchen, and he brought Julia out through the swinging doors with him."

"That's odd," Adam said, sipping his own drink. "I mean, going in through the kitchen I can understand. But why didn't he just head right to the cash register?"

"Maybe he thought grabbing the first person he saw would give him more cover," Eric replied. "But that notion didn't exactly work out to his advantage. I just wonder where he went. If he bled out or even if he is alive somewhere, we'll never find him now."

Adam must have sensed his remorse. "Don't beat yourself up, old man. You shot him in self-defense, and to protect Julia. We can only imagine what he would have done to her if he'd taken her with him." Then he looked down the street where a few cars passed by now and then. "Besides, I'm the one who let him get away."

Eric thought about that. "He must have had help, someone waiting for him." He didn't like the nasty scene playing inside his head. "I don't want to think about that. I just hate—"

"You don't like having to shoot someone. We've all had to deal with that at times."

"What if he just needed some money? Maybe I should have tried to talk him down more."

Adam shook his head. "You saw the man's eyes. He was too far gone. For some strange reason, he picked a bad day to rob the place." Then he shook his head. "And even though we let him get away, he left a trail of evidence—bloodstains on Julia's blouse and fingerprints on both the outside door and the swinging door from the kitchen."

"Got any leads?"

"As a matter of fact, I think we do," Adam said, handing Eric a printout, then added, "Of course, *officially,* I'm not supposed to have this information. So, *unofficially* and just for your information, we had a sketch artist come over from Longview and talk to several of the witnesses, including Julia, Cat and me."

Eric lifted his chin. "Yeah, I gave a description while I was in the hospital, the whole routine. Tell me something I don't know."

Adam tapped the papers he was holding. "Based on the sketch and the fingerprints we were able to lift, we've established his identity. We found some fresh prints on the back door, ran 'em through AFIS and came up with a positive match. We've narrowed it down, based on the eye witness descriptions and the sketch. When we hear from the DNA samples, we'll have it confirmed.

His name is Mingo Tolar, last known address a seedy hotel in El Paso. And he has a record as long as my arm."

Eric read over the sheet, then glanced at the sketch. "Petty theft, drunk and disorderly conduct, disturbing the peace, trespassing and resisting arrest, possession of narcotics. Why does that not surprise me?" Then he shook the rap sheet. "So if this is our man—and this looks exactly like him—how'd he wind up all the way across the state in a tiny town like Wildflower?"

"Maybe he was a mule," Adam replied. "Just passing through on a drug run along the interstate. Maybe he needed some drug money. He might have sampled the goods, panicked, thought he'd better replace the merchandise. He was high when he hit us, so that means he was also careless. We'll know more when the DNA results from the blood drops we found come back from the CODIS lab in Ft. Worth."

"Did we locate a vehicle?"

"Not yet. He either had someone waiting in a getaway car, or he might have hidden until he could run. He was pretty strung out, best I can remember."

"No wonder he was such a loose cannon."

"All the more reason for us to get Julia away from him before he could take off with her." Adam shrugged, shook out the tightness in his muscles. "I just wish I could have caught him. We searched every building around here and immediately sent out patrols. Amazing how he got away so quickly."

Eric nodded, letting the information settle in his gut. Letting a bad guy slip right through their fingers hadn't gone over very well with the department. Reminding himself that he and Adam had at least saved Julia, he shifted on his feet. "Something just isn't sitting right."

"Maybe the fact that I'm stuck on a desk job until this is cleared up, and you're on sick leave for a few more days, or that we're not even supposed to be investigating this thing, period?"

Eric looked around, then shrugged. "We were involved. That tends to make a man curious. And…regardless of whether I'm the *official* investigating officer or not, I need some answers."

Adam slanted a look at him. "Talk to me, brother."

Eric closed his eyes, going over the details one more time in his mind. He thought about Julia's expression, about the man's skittishness, about how she'd silently appealed to Eric to help her. There had been something else there in her eyes, something Eric couldn't quite pinpoint.

But Adam's next words brought it all to the surface. "It's like he went straight for Julia, know what I mean? Almost like the money was an afterthought."

Eric glanced from his friend back into the restaurant. "Yeah, I do know what you mean. And you know what else? It's like Julia Daniels had been expecting someone to do just that."

* * *

She hadn't expected all this attention. The publicity generated from both the newspapers and the television stations had Julia's head throbbing. And had her even more worried that she'd somehow be discovered. It was bad enough, having to give detailed statements to the investigators, then having to describe the man to a sketch artist.

If she only knew what she'd been running from, she might be able to get a better grip on her sanity. Between the ringing phone and the network crews from both Longview to the west and Shreveport to the east in Louisiana, she hadn't had a chance to even do her Saturday chores and errands. And Moria was asking more and more questions.

Julia glanced out the front window, glad to see the camera crews had left. She wasn't giving any more statements. She was done with this.

But as she turned to go do the laundry, she heard a car door slam. Rushing back to the window, she peeked through the blinds to see who was out there now.

Eric Butler.

Julia's heart went into overdrive. What was he doing here? And why hadn't she combed her hair and put on some makeup this morning? Running her hands through her long tresses, Julia decided she didn't care. She had too much to worry about. The good deputy was probably just checking on her out of a sense of duty.

And she did owe him a lot. At least a cup of coffee and a slice of pie.

But when she opened the door, Eric Butler didn't look as if he were in the mood for either. "Hello," Julia said, trying to give him a reassuring smile.

"Hi, yourself. Got a minute?"

"Of course." She waved him into the room. "I'm glad you came by. I've been meaning to come and see you."

He gave her one of his level, steady looks. "Oh, and why is that?"

Julia's heart sent a warning jolt through her system. "Well, to thank you, of course. You most likely saved my life. I…appreciate it."

He waved his good arm in the air. "Don't worry about that." Then he looked into her eyes, his expression as calm and centered as the still American flag hanging on her front porch. "We couldn't let that man take you with him."

"I didn't want to go with him." She turned toward the kitchen. "Want some coffee? Some of Cat's famous apple pie? She brought a fresh one by just this morning."

Silence.

Julia turned to look at him. "Deputy?"

"Call me Eric," he said, lifting a shoulder off the porch post.

"Okay. Eric, would you like some coffee and pie?"

"What I want, Mrs. Daniels, is the truth."

Swallowing back her surprise, she retorted, "Call me Julia."

"Okay. Julia, we need to talk."

Julia could understand how a criminal would be intimidated by this man. He stood almost six feet tall and right now he was all business. "I'm not sure I understand," she said, wondering if he'd already found out about Alfonso's mysterious death. Had he also found out something that would incriminate her? "I've talked to just about everyone in the sheriff's department and the police department. What do we need to discuss?"

Eric took two long strides toward her. "I want you to tell me why that man would have come to Wild-flower…. Looking for you?"

Julia gasped, then shrank back. "I don't…I mean…I didn't know he was looking for me." She sank down on a chair, then stared up at him. "What are you talking about? *Was* he looking for me?"

"That's what I'd like to know," Eric replied, his tone gentle now, his expression relaxing. "I'm just trying to figure this thing out, so it can make some sense. I don't believe this was a routine robbery. Got anything you'd like to share with me about all of this?"

"I didn't know that man, if that's what you're asking," Julia replied, praying Moria would stay in her room a little while longer. She didn't want her daughter to hear this conversation. "I'm telling you the truth. I'd never seen him before. Maybe you need to be honest with me, too, Deputy. If I'm in danger. If my daughter is—"

"I didn't say that." He let out a breath. "We're still

investigating. We've put out an APB based on eye-witness descriptions and our findings, and we have a rap sheet and a positive ID on someone who fits the robber's description. He's a dangerous man, which is why I'm trying—on my own time—to do a more detailed investigation into his background."

"So I don't have to talk to you, since you're not even supposed to be here, right?"

His gaze swept over her face, then back down. "No, you don't have to tell me anything. But...I'm trying to help you here." He glanced at the picture of Moria sitting on the coffee table. "For your daughter's sake, at least."

Julia couldn't tell him to go away after that. "What do you need to know?"

Satisfied that they understood each other, he said, "His name was Mingo Tolar. Ring a bell?"

She shook her head. "No, I'm sorry, it doesn't."

Eric nodded, then pinned her with another level look. "But, did that man happen to know *you?* That's what I'm wondering. And I'm not giving up on this until I find out what's going on. Because if he did know you...if he did come here looking for you, then yes, you and your daughter might still be in danger."

Julia gulped back her fear, her gaze meeting his. He gave her the same steady, reassuring look he'd given her in the restaurant the other day. Then he looked past her into the hallway, his eyes full of surprise.

Julia turned around to find Moria standing there with Rosa clutched to her chest. And a brilliant fear shattering her big brown eyes.

FOUR

Julia rushed to Moria. "Hey, honey. I didn't see you there." Bringing her daughter into the room, she pulled Moria close as she sat down on the couch. "This is my friend Mr. Butler."

Moria sent a big-eyed look toward Eric. "Are we in trouble, Mommy?"

"Now why would you think that?" Julia asked, trying to keep her tone calm. She glanced over at Eric, hoping he hadn't noticed the fear in her child's eyes. Or her own, for that matter.

Moria leaned close, her hands going around Julia's neck. "The policemen came yesterday, just like they did when Daddy went away."

Julia's gaze slammed into Eric's. She could see the questions burning there inside his eyes. Pulling at Moria's long hair with her fingers, she tried to laugh. "Oh, that. Well, it's just that something happened at my work the other day and the police are trying to get information. But you and I haven't done anything wrong. We're okay, honey. It's okay. And Mr. Butler is…he's a sheriff's deputy. That's like a policeman, sorta. And he's just trying to help out."

Moria didn't look convinced. "He scares me. I don't like policemen and I don't like strangers."

Eric's smile was short and quick. "I'm a friend of your mother's. But you're smart to be careful around strangers. Has anyone besides the policemen come by to see you or your mother?"

"No."

"Has anyone who scares you tried to bother you at school or anywhere else, like when you're playing outside?"

Moria shook her head but refused to say anything else.

Julia sent Eric a pleading look. "Can we finish this later?"

His nod was so subtle she almost missed it, but his eyes were on Moria. "You know, I've sure heard a lot about you from your mother. She loves you a lot."

Moria didn't reply, instead she clung to Julia even more. Afraid for her daughter, Julia gently lifted Moria up onto the couch. "Honey, stay right here while I show Mr. Butler out, okay? You can color in that new book I bought you at the grocery store yesterday."

"Okay," Moria said, taking Rosa in her lap. She stared up at Eric with obvious distrust, then went to the small kitchen table where her crayons and coloring book lay.

Julia motioned for him to follow her out onto the porch. After she'd shut the door, she said, "I appreciate your concern, but…Moria doesn't understand what's going on, and I don't know anything about this man. I only know that I was scared, very scared, when he had that gun aimed at my head. And I am so thankful that you helped to get me away from him." Then a new fear penetrated her already frazzled mind. "You don't think he'd come back, do you?"

Eric's gaze moved over her, glassy and unreadable. "That depends. He's wounded and he's wanted for attempted armed robbery, and somehow he managed to get away. He'd need a mighty good reason to come back to Wildflower, don't you think?"

She *thought* he was fishing again, and Julia refused to give him any more information than necessary. "I think he'd be crazy to do that, but…I want to feel safe. I did feel safe here until this happened."

He leaned back against the porch railing, his quiet gaze moving over her face. "Want to tell me about… your past? Where'd you come from?"

"I don't have to answer that."

"Anyone in your past who might want to do you harm?"

She glanced away, then back. Should she tell him the truth? But what purpose would that serve? Until they found this man, if this was the right man, who knew why he'd come to the diner? Maybe it had just been a random robbery and maybe she was just imagining things because of her husband's horrible death. She didn't want to relive all of that unless she had to.

Finally, she said, "I don't think so."

His harsh gaze made her edgy. "But you're not sure?"

Dropping her hands to her sides, she asked, "How can I be sure? I've tried to live a quiet, normal life. I don't have anything to hide. I just need to protect my daughter."

"From what?"

Impatient, she said, "From the press, from the police asking too many questions. I don't want Moria to worry about me. She's been through enough."

He latched on to that. "Because?"

Letting out a sigh, Julia said, "Her father died last year, okay? Surely you've heard I'm a widow and she's lost her father. We're both still trying to cope with that, but Moria is having a very hard time. I moved here to start over and to help her get through her grief. I just didn't need this on top of everything else. So could you just go, please?"

He stepped back, palms up. "I understand and I'm sorry. Did you tell—"

"I told the sheriff's investigators, the police officer who questioned me yesterday, and...Cat knows, of course. I didn't tell the newspapers and television crews that my daughter has horrible nightmares about losing her father, because it's none of their business. Can we just leave it at that?"

"They'll keep digging."

"I'm afraid of that." She ran her hands through her hair. "And I know you can keep digging. You are a lawman, after all. You can find out anything you want about me. Which means I'll probably have to pack up and move again."

He went on full alert now. "Why would you do that?"

Wishing he hadn't pushed her so much, she let out a bitter laugh. "I just want to get on with my life, and I thought I'd be able to do that here. But I won't have my daughter being harassed because I happened to be in the wrong place at the wrong time."

He lifted off the railing then, his eyes moving over her with suspicion and concern. "Or…maybe you were the right person in the right place at precisely the right time. Maybe that robber knew exactly where you were and how to get to you. Which is why, if you have anything else you'd like to tell either me—off the record—or the official investigators for the record, you'd better do it, and quick. Or you *won't* be able to protect yourself or your daughter."

With that he turned to leave. But he stopped on the steps to look back at her, then pulled a card out of his shirt pocket to shove toward her. "Take this. And call me if you need anything. Anything at all, okay?"

Julia took the card, her fingers moving over the etched lettering that included his name and work number. "Thank you."

"My home number and cell are written on the back," he added. "Again, off the record since technically I'm off the case."

She turned it over to scan the scrawled numbers. "Are you always this prepared?"

"I do my homework, yeah."

That sounded like a warning. As in, he wasn't going to give up on this. And how could she expect him to? The authorities were trying to find a man who had tried to commit armed robbery. And she was caught right in the middle. It only made sense that every area of her life would be scrutinized and analyzed until they found some answers. But…she wasn't the criminal, she reminded herself. She just prayed they'd find the man and this would end before she had to bare her past to all of them.

"I hope you find that man," she said as he headed down the steps. "And I'm sorry I couldn't help you more."

He turned one last time, his fingers on the door of his car. "And I hope you learn to trust me, so *I* can help *you*."

Julia watched as he got in a big black truck and drove away. Could she trust him? She remembered how she'd looked toward him the day of the robbery. His strength had given her courage. The connection she'd felt that day as their eyes had locked had stayed with her, making her think she had found a champion. But she was still afraid to tell him the truth. *What should I do, Lord?*

It was just too dangerous, too risky. Or was she afraid of more than her past? If she poured out her heart to Eric Butler, she could lose a part of herself all over again, the way she had with Alfonso. And she refused to give control of her life to another person ever again. She wanted to be the one in charge this time around. And that meant protecting her child.

Julia went inside where Moria had her coloring book and crayons out on the kitchen table. "Want a snack, honey?"

Moria bobbed her head. "Is that big man gone?"

Julia had to smile at that description. Eric Butler did cast a tall shadow. "Yes, he's gone." She sat down across from Moria. "Mr. Butler is one of the good guys, Moria. He's very nice and he works hard to help people every day. You don't have to be afraid of him, okay?"

"Okay." Moria's dark eyes looked solemn and unsure. "I wish he could have helped Daddy."

"Me, too, honey," Julia said. "Me, too."

"Will that nice man keep them away?"

Julia's heart went still at her daughter's innocent question. "Keep who away, darling?"

"You know, the mean people."

Wondering if Moria was beginning to remember something, Julia tried not to show the terror holding her heart like a vise. "What mean people, Moria?"

Moria kept right on coloring the picture of flowers in a big basket. "The ones I heard that night Daddy and I played hide and seek. They were shouting."

Julia put a hand to her mouth, then pursed her lips to fight the chills moving up and down her spine. "Do you know what they were saying?"

Moria shook her head. "It was angry voices. Loud, angry voices. They sounded rude."

Julia watched as her daughter seemed to shut back down right in front of her eyes. "I'm sorry you had to hear that. We don't allow rude voices, do we?"

Moria kept on coloring, bearing down until Julia noticed that one of the flowers was now a darker pink than all the others. And then, the crayon snapped from the pressure. Julia gasped at the sound, then saw the pain in her daughter's dark eyes.

"I broke the violet one," Moria said, tears brimming over onto her cheeks. "It's my favorite."

Julia rushed to hug her daughter close. "We'll fix it, honey."

Moria began to sob. "It can't be fixed."

Julia's eyes filled with their own hot tears as she hugged her daughter close. Maybe Moria was right; maybe this couldn't be fixed.

Unless she went to the one man who'd offered to help her. Maybe it was time she did learn to trust Eric Butler.

Eric stared out at the quiet, still waters of Caddo Lake, his thoughts swirling right along with the slow-moving water. Julia Daniels was obviously hiding something, but what? And why was it so important that he find out?

Hearing footsteps on the dock behind him, he turned to find his father strolling toward him, two plastic cups of ice tea in his hands. All around them, the bald cypress trees stood silent and watchful, their moss-draped branches drooping toward the water. "Need a drink, son?"

"Sure," Eric said as Harlan made his way across the sturdy wooden deck. "How'd you know I was thirsty?"

"Just figured," Harlan replied, handing Eric his tea. "How's the shoulder doing?"

"Better," Eric said, taking his drink with his free hand. "Still throbs now and then, but I think I'm gonna make it."

"Never doubted it," Harlan said on a chuckle. "Fish biting?"

Eric glanced at his forgotten pole, then looked at the cork bobbing below. "I haven't checked the line in about an hour, so I guess not."

"Somehow, I don't think your mind's on fishing," Harlan said. He set his tea on the dock railing, then pulled in the line. "Nothing on here for a fish to nibble, son."

"I guess my heart's not in it today."

"You still pondering this robbery?"

Eric nodded. "She's hiding something. Now I'm wondering—do I keep digging, or do I just leave things alone and let the boys take care of business."

"That might be best," Harlan said. He threw the baited line back into the black water, scaring a lazy turtle off a nearby log. "After all, they're looking for a criminal. But you seem more interested in the victim."

Eric looked up at the tranquil azure sky. The tall cypress trees looked like ancient sentinels, their trunks gray and ghostly in the afternoon shadows. Somewhere off in the distance, he heard a splash, then the sound of wood ducks quacking alone the shore. "I'm just worried, Dad. I think Julia Daniels might be in some sort of danger."

"Because of the robbery?"

He nodded, sipped his sweet tea. "That and the fact that the robbery might have happened because of her being here. Her husband died about a year ago, but she wouldn't say how."

"So you think she might have been a target?"

"I do. But I think they sent the wrong man. This Mingo, he didn't have his act together. If someone sent him to find Julia Daniels, he did that. But he sure messed up on taking her back to them…and I'm pretty sure that's what he was aiming to do." Then he turned to give his father a direct look. "Or maybe he just had orders to kill her."

"That's a bit forward, don't you think?"

"I'm thinking all sorts of things right now." He told Harlan about his conversation that morning with Julia. "The woman was as skittish as a barn cat. And the little girl was afraid of me. I could see it in her eyes."

Harlan stood silent for a while. "What do you make of it?"

Eric didn't want to voice the scenario that kept playing inside in his head. But he knew his father would help him sort through things. "I'm thinking domestic abuse, maybe."

"That would explain Julia's need to keep things quiet. And...bad as it sounds...that would also explain the child's fear. But if the husband was abusive why would someone else be after Julia. Her husband is dead."

"Maybe someone blames her," Eric replied. "Or maybe the in-laws want custody of the child. Who knows." He looked out over the water. "Or...my worst fear...that Julia somehow had something to do with her husband's death, maybe to protect herself and her daughter."

"This could be tricky, son."

Eric finished off his tea. "Yeah, but if they're in danger, I have to do something."

"I know," Harlan said, resolve steeling his words. "I know, son. But...you need to talk to someone down at the station about this. Let them investigate."

Eric didn't like that plan. "I'd rather handle it on my own. So she'll trust me."

Harlan's shrewd gaze hit Eric square in the face. "Son, do you have some sort of feelings for this woman?"

Eric looked back out over the water. "She's just someone who needs my help, I think. Someone who's trying to live her life right, you know what I mean?"

"I do, if she's sincere and not a murderer," Harlan replied.

"I can't picture her being that," Eric said, although that thought had crossed his mind. "I just think she's scared."

"And you think you can help her?"

"I don't know," Eric replied with a shrug. "I only know that for some reason, I can't seem to shake this."

Harlan laid a hand on Eric's arm. "You went down this road once before, remember? You can't save 'em all. That kind of involvement can ruin a lawman."

Eric returned his father's stare with one of his own. "No, but maybe I can save this one, Dad. This one. That's what my gut is telling me."

Harlan let his hand fall, nodded, then turned back to his fishing pole. "Hey, looka here." He tugged on the line, then yanked the pole up. "I think I just caught dinner."

Eric laughed, then shook his head at the small, wiggling catfish. "Figures you'd catch something the minute you threw in. And me, I've been trying for an hour, now, and not a bite."

"The fish were letting you have some thinking time," Harlan shot back. Then he added, "And it sounds like you've got bigger fish to fry, anyway."

Eric had to agree with that. He was going to do a little digging while he was on paid leave. He was going to find out everything he could about Julia Daniels.

Whether she wanted him to know or not.

FIVE

Adam sat down in the worn leather chair facing the sliding glass doors of Eric's log-cabin lake house. "Well, bud, I've got good news and I've got bad news."

Eric shut down the file he'd been reading on the computer screen, then turned to his friend, fatigue settling over him like the sun settling over the water. He'd dug up some interesting things himself. "So do I. You go first."

"We found Tolar," Adam replied, slapping a file down on the coffee table. "Well, *I* didn't find him, but the authorities way across the state did. That's the good news."

Eric hated to even ask. "And the bad?"

"He won't be talking. He's dead. Been dead for about a week, according to the San Antonio investigators."

Eric stood up to stare out at the big, sloping yard and the water beyond. "Dead? In San Antonio?"

"Yep. But, the other good news is that he didn't die from the slug you put in him. He was stabbed. And the other even better news, we've both been cleared to return to full duty—me right now, you whenever the doc tells you you're good to go. And the even better news— they found Tolar's gun. We should be able to match the slug to the weapon, at least. Case solved."

Eric nodded, his teeth biting into his bottom lip, thinking that wouldn't solve what was really bother- ing him. "Tolar was found dead in San Antonio, from a stab wound?"

"That's about the gist of it," Adam replied, a long sigh emitting from deep within. "That bites, doesn't it?"

Eric swung around, glad that they were alone in the big house. His father usually walked across the yard each day to eat dinner with Eric, but tonight Harlan had gone into Longview to eat with some of his fishing buddies. "Sure does, especially when I've just researched a whole lot of interesting things on Julia Daniels."

Adam looked up at him with a squint. "Such as?"

"Such as, she lived in San Antonio for about ten years before she came here. And she used to go by the name Julia Endicott."

"For real?"

Eric nodded. "She was married, but her husband Alfonso died. The official report is that he was working late one night and an intruder broke into the office and killed him."

"But…you got something to add to that?"

"Yep, he was the CFO for the De La Noche produce company." He twirled his ink pen between his fingers.

"And…Julia was briefly considered a prime suspect in his murder. Although it's never been solved, she's been cleared."

Adam let out a whistle. "Wow."

"Yeah, wow," Eric replied, almost understanding Julia's need for anonymity. "Apparently the police put her through the ringer—based on what little I could find out from phone calls and transcripts. The San Antonio boys aren't talking a whole lot."

"Maybe because the Gardonez family has put a lid on things?" Adam asked, musing out loud.

"A very tight lid, apparently."

Everyone in Texas knew about the wealthy San Antonio family that ran a national food conglomerate. The Gardonez family was well-known and powerful, with members ranging from doctors and lawyers to senators and executives. Through the years, they'd branched out to buy up all kinds of companies— anything that had to do with flowers, fruits and vegetables. They ran a clean business and kept a tight rein on their private lives. So mostly nobody messed with them. The head honcho now, however, had married into the family. From what Eric could find, Luke Roderick pretty much ran the entire operation that his in-laws had inherited and nurtured. But the news wasn't all good. There had been some tension within the ranks over the last few years.

Adam tapped a hand on the arm of his chair. "Murdered while at work for the Gardonez clan? That sure doesn't make any sense. That company has some of the tightest security known to man. How did anyone get inside the building and murder Julia's husband?"

"That's what I'd like to know," Eric replied. That and why Julia hadn't told him the truth right from the get-go.

Adam got up and headed to the kitchen. "Can I have a soda?"

"Sure," Eric replied. "Bring me one and we'll go outside on the deck so I can fill you in."

Adam nodded. "Yeah, 'cause I sure need to hear the rest of this story."

Cat sat down across the table from Julia, her dark eyes wide. "I really think you should tell Eric the rest of the story."

"I can't," Julia said, careful to keep her voice low. Moria was just out the back door talking to Mrs. Ulmer while she did some yard work. Since there was no fence between the two yards, Moria had the run of both of them and Cat's huge garden, too. "I don't want to get all caught up in being paranoid again."

"Honey, someone killed your husband and you don't even know the who or the why. Now would be a perfect time to bring the authorities here in on that little tidbit."

Julia touched a finger to the condensation on her glass of lemonade. "I've thought about telling Eric all of it, but what if I'm just imagining things. The police in San Antonio thought I had made it all up—the hang-up calls, the feeling that someone had been inside my home, even being followed—and maybe I did just imagine those things. I don't have any proof that some-one was trying to scare me, and we both know how the police there treated me. What's to say the authorities here won't react in the same way?"

Cat tapped her long red nails against the table. "Well, you sure didn't make up the part about your husband being murdered not ten feet away from your daughter. And Moria didn't make anything up. She was there that night."

"Exactly," Julia said, getting up to pour her tepid tea in the sink. "And that's why I don't want to go back through this. She was just getting to the point of feeling safe again. I don't want to drag her into something that most likely has nothing to do with my past."

"But what if it does?" Cat asked. "That man just showed up here and…well, he came right for you, honey. And now rumors are flying faster than fishing line."

"What kind of rumors?" Julia turned from the win-dow to stare at Cat. "What have you heard?"

"Oh, you know. That you were the target. That the man got away because someone helped him." She shrugged, then lowered her voice. "And something big must have happened today. Adam was in such a mood when he came into the diner. He wouldn't so much as blink any department tips, then he headed right off to find Eric."

Julia's heart thumped a consistent warning. She felt as if her shoulders were wired tight to her neck, the tension in her muscles so flexed it made it hard to breath. "But…we haven't heard anything for over a week. I thought…I thought they were still looking for the robber."

"Oh, they are," Cat said, getting up to help with their dinner dishes. "The other cops and deputies might give up, but Eric and Adam won't rest. This happened to all of us—you, me and them. Not to mention all the other people in the diner that day."

"I'm sorry," Julia said as she dropped dishes into the dishwasher. "I don't want people to think I've brought trouble into Wildflower."

Cat touched a hand to her arm. "Then maybe you need to do something to fix that trouble."

Julia looked at her cousin. "You think this was intentional? You believe this man came here for me?"

"I've just got this feeling," Cat said, rubbing her hands over her arms. "Just like when Nathan went out on that call five years ago. I had this same bad feeling then, too. And I was right. My husband never came back home."

Julia turned to stare out into her backyard, watching as Moria laughed and played with Mrs. Ulmer's tiny Chihuahua, Fred. The wildflowers along the back alley between her house and Cat's were beginning to bloom in vivid blues and lush mauves. Moria was looking forward to the upcoming Wildflower Festival that was held on the town square each year. Julia shut her eyes, trying to imagine what would become of her world if something happened to her daughter.

"Maybe I should just leave," she said, tears pricking at her eyes.

"And go where?" Cat asked. "I'd worry about you day and night. You can't go to your parents in Kentucky. Y'all aren't exactly on speaking terms, as we both know, and they're too old and feeble to take you and Moria in. And besides…you've never been one to just up and run from a fight." Then she looked out at Moria. "And… well…I'd miss you both so much. Having you here has helped me more than you realize."

Julia shook her head. "And you've helped us. But—"

"But nothing," Cat replied. "You can't keep running from something you're not even sure of, Julia. And you *are* safe here, whether you want to believe that or not. Just let Eric help you. Tell him the truth about everything. If you don't want the local law involved, Eric won't bring them in. But he can help you. He's very good at his job. If someone is out there looking for you, Eric will find them before they get to you."

"But what if it's too late?"

Cat looked out the front window. "I don't think it is. Eric and Adam just pulled up in your yard."

"The boss will have our hides for this," Adam said, his expression holding a frown. "The sheriff is already fuming because Tolar got away, and never mind that this is a very small town and he has a pretty good hunch that we haven't been heeding the rules on this already. If he finds out we came over here to talk to Julia before we got the all-clear for full duty tomorrow, we'll be on leave for a very long time."

"I'm on leave *now*," Eric replied. "Nothing in the books says I can't visit a woman's house. And you did get cleared for regular duty today, right?"

"Right, on both. Except that the woman you are visiting is involved in a case where you got shot—a case we're not supposed to be investigating. The sheriff turned it over to his other deputy, remember? And have I failed to mention the Rangers are still involved? We both know how dicey that can be, even if their investigation did clear both of us of any wrongdoing."

"Then why did you bring me this latest information?" Eric asked, slanting his friend a glance as he slammed the truck door shut.

"Because I was trying to be a good friend. I thought you'd like an update—not a date with the woman right in the middle of all this mess."

"Maybe I'm just trying to be a friend, too," Eric retorted.

"Okay, all right," Adam said, a hand in the air. "I see Cat's here. I'll just pretend I came to see her."

"Good idea," Eric replied, "since everyone in town knows you've got a major crush on her."

"Who? Me?" Adam shrugged. "I do not."

"Please," Eric countered. "You're about as subtle as a porcupine."

Adam frowned. "The woman is five years older than me."

"Since when has age stopped you?"

They'd reached the open front door, so Adam couldn't respond. Instead he looked up at the two women staring through the screen at them. "Hey, Cat, Julia. How y'all doing?"

"Out cruising around, boys?" Cat asked, a soft grin forming on her square-shaped face as she gave Adam the once-over.

"Something like that," Adam said, giving her a look that Eric interpreted to mean anything but.

"Can I talk to you?" Eric asked Julia, waiting as she stared at him with open anxiety through the wire separating them.

Julia looked spooked already and he hadn't even told her about Tolar being found dead. Then he glanced at Cat, realization dawning. Cat knew whatever it was Julia was trying so hard to keep a secret. But then, so did he now. Or he knew some of it. Was there more?

"What's this about?" Julia asked, clearly afraid to hear his news, whatever it was.

Adam nodded toward Cat. "Hey, Cat, let's go around back and see how Mrs. Ulmer's tomatoes are coming along. I saw her back there. She could probably use a hand with pulling weeds."

Cat lifted a brow, obviously about to tell him no thanks. But when both Eric and Adam gave her a long, steady look, she took the hint. "Oh, all right. But you know I don't like to sweat."

"Yeah, I know," Adam retorted as he watched her saunter out onto the porch. "But you sure look pretty when you glisten."

"You are such a teaser," Cat replied, sticking her tongue out at him as they headed down the front steps and around the house. Then she called back to Julia, "Take your time. I'll watch Moria."

Eric waited as Julia moved toward him. She seemed in slow motion, as if each step were a struggle.

"You look beat," he said, his gaze moving over her face.

"Thanks," she quipped. "Lack of sleep does that for a girl."

He could see the dark smudges underneath her eyes. "You're having trouble sleeping?"

"Yes, but then, you probably know that. I hear everyone in town is talking about me, speculating on what type of dire things I've brought down on Wildflower."

"Do you think you've brought us trouble?"

"I think," she said, a long shudder of a sigh moving through her as she pushed at her ponytail, "that I need to move on."

"Why?"

"Why?" She glared at him, her eyes going from gold to green like heat lightning at dusk. "Because I'm worried. Moria is so…confused."

"We can get her help. We can get both of you help."

They moved through the front yard. Eric purposely took her away from the house, so no one would listen to their conversation. "Do you hear me?"

She gave him a look of resolve, but her standoffish demeanor showed her hesitation. "I hear you. We've had help. And I've already taken her to therapists in both Marshall and Longview. I know what I need to do for my little girl. She misses her father, she has nightmares, and she seems to cling to the things he gave her. Sometimes she even hides the few special gifts Alfonso gave her. She tells me they used to play hide-and-seek at our other house. Then she'd pick special things around the house to hide, and Alfonso would try to find them. She still does that sometimes." Eric saw the shiver she tried to suppress. "I don't like playing hide-and-seek anymore."

He leaned against the bumper of his truck, then turned to look into her eyes. "Why didn't you tell me your husband was murdered?" He wanted to add "And that you were a suspect?" But he kept that information to himself for now.

Her gasp of shock didn't surprise him. "How did you—" Then she shook her head, her eyes full of distrust and disappointment. "Never mind. Stupid question."

"I've had a lot of time on my hands," he said by way

of an explanation. "I did my own background check. Alfonso Endicott—thirty-five years old, successful CPA—head of accounting with the De La Noche produce company, San Antonio, Texas. Mother, Regina, now lives in San Juan, Mexico. Father was a successful Texas businessman, but died from cancer about a year before Alfonso was killed. Murderer was never found and no motive other than a random robbery was ever established."

"Are you finished?" she asked, her hands shaking, her eyes flashing. "Are you satisfied?"

"No, I'm not finished," he said. Then he leaned toward her. "And I'm sure not satisfied."

"I'm going to leave this place," she said, wiping at her eyes. "I can't deal with this."

"Where will you go?"

"My folks…live in Kentucky. They're retired and they have a lot of health issues, but I'll go there. I should have gone there to begin with. I can help them. They need my help, but they insist on trying to be independent."

Eric heard her trying to convince herself, but he wasn't buying it. "Why do you have to leave, Julia?"

She crossed her arms, her whole stance defiant. "You mean you haven't figured that out yet?"

"I think I might have a hunch," he said, hoping she'd just go ahead and tell him. "Are you afraid because your husband was murdered? Did he abuse you?"

Shock once again colored her face. "Alfonso? Abuse me? No…it wasn't like that. Alfonso didn't have a mean bone in his body. He was a hard worker and a good husband. He loved his family. But he also loved his job, too much." Shaking her head, she said, "It wasn't abuse. Nothing like that."

Relief pulsed like fast-moving water through Eric's system. "I thought maybe—"

Then she gasped, realizing what had been worrying him all along. "That I'd killed my husband, or had him killed?" Putting a hand to her mouth, she moaned low in her throat. "I loved him. He was the sweetest man in the world, and he tried to give me the world. *That's* what killed him."

She came around the truck, then sank against the passenger side, her hands on her knees. Glancing up and down the street, she said, "I'm afraid for my daughter." Then she turned to look at him. "Moria was in the building the night Alfonso was killed."

Eric felt as if he'd been gut-punched. Sucking in a breath, he said, "I did not know that."

"Not many people do." She glanced toward the sounds of laughter coming from the backyard. "The police kept it very quiet, to protect her, and to save the Gardonez family any further publicity, of course. We…we weren't sure what she saw or heard that night."

Eric didn't like the ugly scene playing inside his head. "Where was she?"

"In a bathroom, with Alfonso's cell phone. He'd dialed my phone for her and told her to stay right there and tell Mommy to come quick. She thought it was all another game of hide-and-seek."

"And when you got there?"

"I had someone call the police while I stayed on the line with her, but by the time I got there, about ten minutes later, they had already found Alfonso. He'd been stabbed several times." She gulped, closed her eyes. "Moria was sitting in a chair in the women's bathroom, playing with her doll."

Eric came around the truck to hold her, only because she looked as if she might collapse right there in the street. "I'm sorry. No wonder you're so on edge. So this is why you refused to tell us about your background."

"I don't know what to do," she said, tears streaming down her face. "I don't know if Tolar was after me…or Moria. Or maybe both of us. Eric, I'm telling the truth. I don't know what happened that night, and I don't know if Tolar was here because of me."

Eric pulled her close, the sweet scent of her shampoo clashing with the bitter tone of his words. "You don't have to worry about Tolar anymore. He's dead."

Julia drew back, shock coloring her pale face. "Are you sure?"

He nodded. "Yep. But…Julia, he didn't die from the shoot-out during the robbery. They found him in San Antonio, in a back alley. He'd been stabbed repeatedly."

She looked up at him, her eyes wide with horror and doubt. "Just like Alfonso. Who? Why?"

"We don't know."

Her next words were barely above a whisper. "Is it over, then?"

Eric couldn't lie to her. He held her, steadying her. Then he said, "No, I think it's just beginning. I think whoever killed Tolar will send someone else to finish the job. And that means you're still in danger."

Julia slumped back against the truck. "I can't go through this again. This can't be happening."

"But it is happening," Eric said, his hand on her chin so she was forced to look him in the eye. "And you can't keep running. If Tolar has some sort of connection to your husband's murder, then it's even more dangerous now that he's dead. Whoever is behind this will only send someone else to find you. You've got to level with me, Julia. Right now. I need to know everything you know, so I can help you. Before it's too late."

SIX

The next morning Julia stood in the kitchen at the Courthouse Café, remembering the day a few months after Alfonso's death when she'd called Cat to ask if she could come and visit. Cat had immediately picked up on her anxiety.

"Come and *live* here," Cat had suggested. "And if you need work, well, I can always use another waitress. You worked here when we were teens. I'm thinking you can work here again. Just until you decide what you want to do." When she'd offered her deceased grandmother's vacant house, as well, Julia had taken that as a sign that her prayers had been answered.

So Julia had sold off all the fancy designer furnishings and the big house in San Antonio, taking that money and the insurance settlement to start a new life here in the quiet piney woods of East Texas.

She had certainly thought about going back to Kentucky, just to get as far away from Texas as possible.

But Cat's offer has seemed like a good place to start, since her parents had practically disowned her when she'd married Alfonso. They hadn't appreciated the way the Texan had come to town and swept their daughter off her feet. Maybe they'd seen something in her future husband that she'd been too blind to see.

Whatever it was, her parents hadn't reached out to her since she'd left Kentucky, not even after she'd become a widow with a child. They came for the funeral and they kept in touch, but they didn't visit at all. They sent Moria Christmas and birthday presents, but anything beyond that was strained and awkward. So she'd settled here in this beautiful, quiet little town, hoping for a new start.

She and Cat had always been close, and Cat understood her need to be independent, to do things her own way. Cat would come if Julia called, but she wasn't overbearing or pushy. She was a relative, but she was also a good friend.

Which was why it would be so hard to leave. But after talking to Eric yesterday, she didn't have a choice. She was scared—scared of this threat looming over her head and scared of the way she wanted to give in to her need to depend on Eric Butler for help.

Julia turned to stare out the kitchen window toward the back alley. Even there, where few people needed to venture, Cat had planted a climbing rosebush against a white trellis. The tiny red roses were budding all over the place in anticipation of the long summer days ahead.

But she wouldn't be here for that, Julia decided. She'd

only come in today to give her notice and collect her check. She wouldn't risk Moria's safety by staying in Texas, no matter how much she loved living in Wildflower. No matter how much Eric Butler had promised to help her.

She heard the swinging door fly open, then turned to find Cat standing there, her hands on her hips. "So you're bailing out on me, huh?"

Julia shook her head. "I've caused enough trouble. I don't want to bring more down on you."

"I can take care of myself," Cat said, a scowl on her face, her lone-star earrings dancing. "And I'm pretty sure among all of us around here, we can take care of you and Moria, too."

Julia turned back to stare at the climbing roses. A sparrow landed on the trellis, hopping back and forth along the tiny ledge at the top. "But you shouldn't have to look over your shoulder, wondering if someone else will come searching for us."

Cat let out an unladylike snort. "Jul, I'm surrounded by lawmen here. I was married to one. I'm always looking over my shoulder."

"But…this isn't fair to you, this having to watch out for me, too," Julia retorted. "I'll just go back home to Kentucky. For a little while, at least."

Cat tilted her head. "So…your solution to all of this is just to keep on moving around? What kind of life is that? And what about your parents? Won't you be putting them in danger, too?"

Anger poured over Julia as thick and heavy as the maple syrup they served with the pancakes each morning. "It's the only life I have right now. These people—"

"You don't know who they are," Cat said, hitting her hand against the stainless steel counter. "You don't know for sure that they're after you or Moria."

"I know that man—Tolar—was murdered in San Antonio. That's all I need to know."

"Honey, he was a thug. He messed with the wrong people."

"But…he wound up in San Antonio for some reason. Why did he end up there of all places?"

Cat shrugged, then turned to start dragging out the supplies for the day. "I can't answer that. But it sure doesn't make a bit of sense for you to just up and leave because of it. Why don't you let the sheriff and his men do their jobs, then decide what's best."

Julia ran a hand through her hair. "I can't take that chance, Cat. Not when my child is involved."

Cat yanked down bowls and grabbed at utensils, her actions making a lot of noise. The cook who'd been with the café for over twenty years rolled his eyes as he hurried by with a carton of eggs. The early-shift waitresses gave Cat a wide berth as they clipped their orders on the wire over Cat's head. Even a few of the early-morning regulars glanced up from their coffee and toast.

"Hey, what's all the commotion back there?"

Both women looked out of the open pass-through to find Eric standing at the counter. "Hey, there," Cat said, turning to give Julia a long, hard look. "I was just trying to convince my stubborn cousin here to hold her horses before she goes running off to the wild blue yonder."

Julia glared at Cat, then pushed through the swinging door. "Can I get you something, Deputy?"

"Whoa, somebody got up on the wrong side of the bed," Eric said, but he wasn't smiling. "Will you sit down and have a cup of coffee with me?"

Julia looked from him to Cat. "I…I'm not working today. I just came by to give my notice and collect my last check."

Eric was still wearing a sling, but he managed to lift his fingers in the air toward her. "You can't leave town, Julia."

Julia's mood went from bad to worse. "And why not?"

"Well, this case is still active as far as I'm concerned. In fact, Adam and I just got word yesterday that we're cleared for full duty again. But until I get my doctor's consent to go back, I intend to keep digging on my own. Even though Tolar is dead, we're still trying to figure this thing out, and we need you around for that."

"So you're going to force me to stay on a technicality?"

"I can't force you to do anything, but it would be wise for you to keep a low profile until we know you're safe."

"I can do that—far away from here," she replied. Then she grabbed her purse from behind the counter. "Cat, I'll be back later for my check. I have some packing to do."

Cat let out a groan. "Eric, talk some sense into her, will you?"

Eric lifted his chin toward Cat, then grabbed Julia by the arm. "C'mon."

She halted, pulling away. "I told you, I have to go."

"You're going all right. With me."

"But—"

"Is Moria in school?"

"Yes, but—"

"Good, then we have the whole day." He didn't give her time to argue. He just pulled her through the café and out the front door until he'd reached his truck. Opening the passenger-side door, he said, "Get in. We're going for a little ride."

Julia didn't know what to do. He had a look about him that told her it would be useless to try and get away. "I could scream," she said, determination giving her strength.

"Go right ahead," he replied. "People will just think I'm hauling you in for bad behavior."

She watched as he slammed the door then came around the truck, his expression full of dare and thunder. Her mouth was still open in shocked silence when he cranked the truck and spun out onto the street.

* * *

Eric didn't know why this woman infuriated him so much. But she seemed determined to sabotage any form of help or hand-out, so he decided he could be just as stubborn as her and twice as mean. He wasn't used to man-handling women, but this one needed a good talking-to.

And he was just the man to do it, since he couldn't work because of his injury, and because all he could think about was her and this bad situation.

"You need to take me to my car," Julia said, her voice shaky in spite of the defiant tilt of her chin.

"Not just yet."

He kept driving until they were out of town and moving past the lake. He didn't stop until he was at his cabin.

"Where are we going?" she asked, craning her neck to see the house and the woods. "I don't like this."

Eric didn't bother to answer. He just parked the truck, then got out and came around to her side. When he opened the door, he was met with a steely golden-green glare.

"I'll just call someone to come and get me," she said as she slid off the seat.

"Try it." He knew not even Cat would bother them now. "You refused to talk to me yesterday when I told you about Tolar. But today's different. You're thinking about leaving and that would be a really bad mistake."

"What do you want?" she said, screaming out the words, the echo scaring a pair of mourning doves out of the nearby bushes.

"I want to help you," he said. "But you seem dead set against that notion." He held a hand in the air. "For the life of me, I can't understand why a woman who strikes me as smart would want to take off and put herself and her child in even more danger."

"I just want to leave," she replied, her arms crossed, her booted foot hitting the dirt. Then she seemed to go limp. "I just need to leave."

"That could be very dangerous," he said, inhaling one calming breath as he repeated himself. "You don't know what's waiting out there."

"But I sure can see what's right here—you badgering me, the press hounding me, and…someone obviously sent that man to do me in. I can't stay here, Eric. They know where I am now."

"You can't go, either," he said. "And for that very same reason."

She stared him down for a full minute, then said, "So what do you suggest?"

Relief washed through him. "Now that's better. Are you willing to listen to me?"

"I don't know," she said, shrugging. "I just don't know who I can trust right now."

He touched his free hand to her arm. "Look, we can start from the beginning. We can start with your marriage and everything you can remember about your husband—his work, his social connections, anything or anybody. We need to figure out why he was murdered. And then we'll figure out why you're so afraid."

She looked up at him, all the hostility gone from her eyes. She looked sad and defeated. "Why are you doing this?"

Eric chuckled, then looked out at the dark waters of Caddo Lake. "You know, I keep asking myself that question."

"You could get into trouble with the sheriff. I've heard he's already read you and Adam the riot act for endangering everyone in the café that day."

"Honey, I'm always in trouble with my boss. So just put that notion out of your mind."

"Do you think I'm lying to you?"

"Are you?"

She shook her head. "No, but…honestly, I don't hold out much hope on this. The police in San Antonio didn't believe me."

"What didn't they believe?"

She turned toward the lake. Eric took that as a sign she was ready to talk, so he grabbed her by the elbow and guided her toward the back of the cabin and the deck out over the water. "This is my place. You're safe here." He pointed to the smaller cabin a few hundred feet from his big sprawling cedar one behind them. "That's my dad's place, and I live here in this one. Let's go sit."

She nodded but kept quiet as her gaze moved across the grounds and the water.

"Do you want something to drink?"

She shook her head.

Eric guided her toward two lounge chairs centered on the big deck. "Here."

She sank down across from him, appearing waiflike in her jeans and light sweater. Then she looked over at him. "You don't need to baby-sit me."

"I'm not doing that," he retorted. Then he leaned up in his chair. "I *like* you, okay? I really like you. And I hate to see you so worried. And I sure don't want you to leave Wildflower."

She slanted her head, her gaze touching on him with a hesitant smile. "You *like* me?"

"Yes, I do. I had even thought about asking you out before all of this happened. So just consider this a date."

That made her laugh. "Being practically kidnapped and taken to a remote location to be interrogated? That's your idea of a date? It's a first, I have to admit."

"We could have lots of firsts together," he countered, holding her gaze. "That is, if you stick around long enough to get to know me. And if you allow me to get to know you."

"What do you want to know?" she asked, her eyes going soft.

Eric considered that question a victory. But he knew he had a lot of battles to go before he'd won this war.

* * *

Two hours later Julia had told Eric Butler everything she could remember about Alfonso and the company he worked for. She didn't know if it was the tranquil waters of Caddo Lake, or the calm way in which he managed to question her without making her feel cornered, but she poured it all out to him—all the horror and pain of the last year, all the nights she'd sat up with her daughter, holding Moria because neither one of them could sleep. She'd told him all about the police investigation, the counselors and social workers who'd tried to help Moria remember, and she'd told him all about how Alfonso worked so hard at times that he'd just come home and collapse on the couch and stay there all night.

"We were happy when we first came back to Texas," she said now, as they walked back toward the truck. "It's just that…he had worked for the company since high school, and they'd put him through college, then kept moving him up in the chain of command. It was his life. He was very loyal to the family because his father had also worked there—as a truck driver. Mr. Endicott wanted more for his son, though. So Alfonso became a part of the inner circle. But something was bothering him toward the end. I don't know if he was under too much stress, or if he just had this big weight on his shoulders and he didn't know how to get rid of it."

"But from everything you'd said, the Gardonez family was good to him?"

"Yes. He loved his job. They paid him a generous salary and we lived a good life in a nice neighborhood. We attended church with the family. I just can't believe anyone in that family could have been involved in his murder. That doesn't make any sense." She glanced up as a hawk circled over the tree line. "De La Noche is a solid company, with produce distribution all over the world. Not to mention the nurseries and flower shops. That's how we met—he'd come to Kentucky to oversee an opening for a new distribution center. They trusted him. They were very generous, especially with people as loyal as Alfonso."

Eric followed her gaze on the hawk. They both watched as the graceful bird dived to catch his prey. "Maybe someone else within the company—someone not related to the family?"

Julia thought of Luke Roderick, but she blocked that out of her mind. Even if he'd seemed condescending and superior at times, Luke was a member of the family; he knew the Gardonez way of life and, to his credit, he'd worked hard to rise to the top spot within the company. There was no need to tell Eric that Luke was also a womanizer and that Alfonso had been jealous at the way his married boss hovered around Julia. "I can't think of anyone."

"And what about your suspicions regarding Moria? You do believe that she might have heard or seen something that night?"

"Yes, I feel that in my heart, even if the police never took me seriously. But…she's not talking. I can't prove anything, but right after his death, I just had this feeling that whoever killed Alfonso was still after us."

"And now do you think Tolar came looking for you?"

She nodded. "I didn't want to believe that at first, but I think it's obvious now." Then she looked over at him, her hand on the truck door. "You knew that the day it happened, didn't you?"

Eric didn't even try to deny it. "I could sense something wasn't right, yes. But…I had no idea just how wrong it would turn out to be." Then he rubbed a hand down his jaw. "And you're not alone in your concerns. Nobody back at the sheriff's office except Adam knows or even suspects this link between Tolar and you, not yet anyway. I didn't want to say anything until I confirmed some of this with you. The boss doesn't always move on just my gut instincts alone."

"Cat told me you have good instincts," she said. Then she smiled. "She said you're sensitive, but you don't like to let that show."

He grinned, the strain of the past few hours disappearing from his face. "That would certainly ruin my reputation."

Julia was just about to tell him how much she appreciated his sensitive side when her cell phone rang. She hurriedly dug it out of her purse. "Hello?"

"Julia, this is Mrs. Ulmer. I was just worried about you, darling."

"Why? What's wrong?" Julia immediately thought of Moria. "Did the school call?"

"No, no. But…something funny is going on over at your house. I heard Fred barking out on our screen porch and when I went out to have a look-see, I saw a fellow nosing around over there at your place, so I asked him if I could help him."

Julia held a hand up for Eric to wait. "What did he want?"

"He said he was there to repair the cable or something like that, but after I questioned him, he took off on foot. I just wanted to check."

Julia glanced toward Eric. "I'll be there as soon as I can." She hung up, her pulse echoing at a dangerous pace inside her head. "Mrs. Ulmer said there's a man snooping around my house. I need to go—"

"I'll get you home," he said, hurrying around the truck. After slamming the door, he turned to Julia. "Buckle up. I'll be breaking the speed limit."

"I can't believe this," she said, a sick kind of dread pooling inside her stomach. "I have to go to the school. Eric, I have to find Moria."

"We'll send someone to get her," Eric said, his gaze brooding. "You're going to be okay, Julia. Both of you. I intend to see to that personally."

Julia held on as he sped along the country road

toward her house. She wanted to believe him, because
for the first time in a long time, someone was willing to
believe in her. And for that reason alone she knew she
couldn't run this time. Even though she wanted to.

She asked God to give her the strength to stay and
fight this until it was resolved, one way or another. And
she prayed Eric was right, that he could help her.

"What exactly did Mrs. Ulmer say?" Eric asked.

She filled him in, then said, "He told her he was a cable
guy. But I didn't call anyone from the cable company."

Eric gave her a grim look, then gunned the engine.

SEVEN

"Cat's checking Moria out of school right now," Julia told Eric. "She talked to the resource officer on duty and explained we had a possible threat, so he's waiting with Moria."

They'd reached her house in record time. Eric slammed on the brakes and put the truck in Park then hopped out to come around for her. "She'll be okay, then. The school knows Cat is listed in case of an emergency right?"

"Yes, thank goodness," Julia said, her breath catching in her throat. "I just need to see Moria to be sure, but they're going back to the café for now."

Eric guided her up the steps to her house. "Good idea. Moria doesn't need to be here until we find out what's going on."

Julia understood. "As long as I know she's safe—"

Mrs. Ulmer was waiting on her front porch, and now she came rushing over, leaving her husband there to watch from his scooter chair, Fred barking and dancing around by his side. "I'm so sorry for scaring you, Julia. But I declare, when I looked out my back window and saw a strange man coming out of your back door, well, I just knew something wasn't right. Gus heard me calling out to the man, so he naturally wanted to go over there and confront him, but I told him no. We didn't see any type of repair truck, either. That's when I called you."

"Is he still in there?" Eric asked, his voice low.

"I don't know," Mrs. Ulmer said, her lips pursed. "One minute he was there on the porch and the next, he seemed to just disappear around the other side of the house. I didn't get a very good look at him, either. I think Fred's barking scared him off."

"Thanks, Miss Nina," Julia said, her hand on the door.

Eric tugged her back. "Let me go in first."

She nodded, hoping against hope that there truly was some sort of repairman inside her house. But when Eric opened the door, he was immediately met with some resistance. Frowning, he pushed hard until he almost fell into the room.

And that's when both Julia and Mrs. Ulmer gasped at the sight before them. Julia's house had been ransacked. Furniture and magazines were scattered all over the place. A huge sofa pillow was shoved against the door. Even the tiny television had been thrown to the floor.

"Oh, my," Nina Ulmer said, her plump hands going to her mouth. "I should have called the police the minute I saw him. At least Eric is here now."

"Stay out here," Eric warned. "I'm just going to go in and check things out."

"Should I call for help?" Mrs. Ulmer asked in a shaky voice.

Eric looked at Julia. He must have seen her anxiety, since she was shaking all the way from her head to her toes.

"No, not yet. I doubt he's still here. Just stay out here and be quiet. I'll be fine."

Julia wasn't so sure about that. "But your shoulder—"

"I'm well enough to put up a fight," he retorted, his finger going to his mouth to quiet her. "Just stay back."

Julia did as he told her, her hand grabbing Mrs. Ulmer's. Nina waved to her frowning husband to reassure him, even if neither of them felt all that reassured themselves.

Then Nina picked up a small garden shovel Julia had left on the porch. "Take this, at least."

Eric frowned but took it, then he pushed inside the door. "Wait right here."

While they waited, Julia held her breath and asked God to help her. It had been a while since she'd turned to God for any favors or pleas. Probably since the night the police had told her that her husband was dead. Not once during all her fears and trepidation in San Antonio had she relied on God to calm her or guide her. But standing here, in this rental house in Wildflower, with the sun shining in a piercing deception of peace and tranquility all around her, she knew she needed God's help in dealing with this. And she was beginning to believe God was sending her that help in the form of one very brave hero.

"I pray Eric doesn't find anything bad in there," Mrs. Ulmer said.

Julia nodded. "So do I." And this time she meant it.

When her phoned beeped, she almost jumped out of her skin. "Julia, it's Cat. Moria is at the café with me and Adam is staying close. Is everything all right at home?"

"I don't know. Eric's checking it out. Someone broke into my house."

"Oh, honey, that's not good. I'll keep Moria here until I get the all-clear from you, all right?"

"All right. I'll call you." She heaved a breath. "And Cat, please keep an eye on her."

"You know I will. She can help me make the pies for tomorrow's lunch crowd."

Julia closed the phone just as Eric emerged from inside her ruined living room. "He's not in here. He must have been leaving when you spotted him, Nina. Your dog must have spooked him, so he tried to get away without anyone seeing him." He gave the older woman a gentle look. "Do you think you could identify this man?"

Nina shook her head. "I don't know, Eric. I didn't have on my glasses."

Eric nodded. "We'll worry about that later then."

Both women let out the breaths they'd been holding.

"I'll go tell Gus what's going on," Mrs. Ulmer said. Then she turned around, her paisley printed apron flying out. "I'll come back and help you clean up, suga'."

"Don't touch anything. I have to call this in first," Eric said, his gaze resting on Julia. "I have to."

She knew what that meant. Even more scrutiny on her private life. But…she really didn't have a choice now. Someone was obviously searching for something. Her husband had died because of this. Mingo Talor had possibly died because of this. She didn't want to think about what these people would do next.

"I know," she told Eric as she stepped inside the clutter of her home. "I know. I just wish—"

"Look, I'm going to Sheriff Whitston with all of this." When Julia held up a hand in protest, he added, "And since I'm not clear for full duty until my arm heals, I'm going to ask him to assign *me* to *you*."

"What?" Julia shook her head. "I don't need a body-guard, Eric."

"Yes, you do. I think you and Moria are being targeted, Julia. And until we find out why and by whom, you need protection."

"So you're just going to camp out on my doorstep?"

"No, not exactly," he said, his gaze sweeping over the broken dishes and strewn food in her kitchen. "But you *are* going to be with me 24/7. You and Moria are coming to stay at the lake with Dad and me. And that's final."

* * *

Later that afternoon Julia was once again on the big deck stretching out over Caddo Lake, the silhouette of Eric's spacious cabin behind her as she allowed the gentle spring wind to play through her hair. Too numb to think about how most of the few possessions she'd brought from San Antonio were now destroyed, she just thanked God that Moria was safe. At least she'd stored some of her more prized possessions in Cat's big attic.

Of course, she'd had to dig in her heels with Eric. She wasn't going to stay out here on the lake day and night, and *that was final,* she'd informed him earlier. However, she was willing to come out here for dinner tonight, just to keep Moria from seeing their house. Cat had agreed to let Julia and Moria stay with her for as long as they needed. After all, Cat had reminded her, she'd wanted them to stay with her when they moved back, anyway, but Julia had insisted that would be imposing. Now Julia felt trapped between two very dynamite forces—her cousin and the man who kept coming to her rescue. They'd reached a compromise of sorts, at least. When she wasn't working at the café, she and Moria would be with either Cat or Eric, or both if need be. They wouldn't be alone until Eric could make sure they were safe again.

"I like it here, Mommy," Moria said from her spot near the railing. "I like the turtles. Do we get to stay a long time?"

"I'm not sure, honey," Moria replied, careful to keep her tone light. "Probably just for dinner, okay?"

Moria nodded. "Why can't we go back home?"

Julia would like to know the answer to that question herself. "I don't know yet. Remember I explained how some things had been damaged at our other house. We have to get that fixed first. We'll visit with Eric and his dad, then we'll stay with Aunt Cat for a while. It'll be fun, since you're out for spring break next week."

Moria clung to her doll. "Rosa likes it here, too."

"I'm so glad," Julia said, turning to touch a finger to the doll's glistening hair.

At least Moria's favorite toy hadn't been destroyed by the burglar. Eric seemed to think the man had heard Fred barking, or something else had alerted him before he'd searched the whole house. Then when he'd seen Mrs. Ulmer, he'd run off. Julia's room had been plundered, but it looked as if the man had stopped midway and left. Moria's bedroom was untouched.

"That just means they'll be back again," Eric had reasoned earlier after the whole place had been dusted for prints.

Hearing footsteps on the deck, she turned now to find him coming toward them, a look of fatigue shadowing his face. Whispering low, he said, "We'll have to wait to hear on the prints—if there were any new ones.

That's all we have to go on right now. Whoever did this, they didn't leave behind any evidence."

"That doesn't surprise me," Julia said. "I have a feeling whoever is behind this is desperate."

Eric leaned close. "Exactly. Even more reason to take extra precautions."

Moria ran up to Eric. "Mr. Eric, I've seen six turtles so far. No alligators, though."

"I wouldn't count on seeing an old gator," he said, running a hand over Moria's head as he stepped close. "They like to lay low. Just remember what I told you—don't ever go out to the dock by yourself, okay?"

"Okay," Moria said, looking back out at the water. "I won't."

Eric's smile was indulgent. "Supper is almost ready."

"I could have helped," Julia said, feeling awkward and out of place with nothing to occupy her time.

"Dad doesn't allow anyone near when he's making his famous chili dogs." He grinned over at Moria. "Hope you like tator tots."

"I love them," Moria replied, her smile shy.

Eric looked back at Julia. "Everything is set. Dad and I both are on active watch now. One of us will be with you or near you at all times. The school has been alerted and they know the routine. You are the only person who can give approval to check out Moria until this is resolved. Nobody else, not even Cat, not even me, you hear? It's important to stick to your routine, no matter how hard that is."

"Then why did I have to leave my home?" she said on a low whisper.

"Because your home is uninhabitable right now. And because you're much safer out here where I have a built-in security system, and a bulldog of a daddy. We'll keep you here and at Cat's house, with Dad, Adam and me taking shifts. The normal routine will begin again once school starts back after spring break. But hopefully, between the authorities in San Antonio, and with our department here working on things, this will be cleared up by then."

Trying to find some humor, she shrugged. "And here I thought this was just your way of getting to know me better."

"Maybe that's part of it, too." His expression changed from amused and interested to deadly serious. "I need to keep you safe and it's just easier on everyone to do that here as much as we can. We're off the beaten path, and we have more room, more distractions for Moria, and…as I said—my dad as backup."

She nodded. "Don't worry. I understand. But I'm going back to Cat's house each night. I don't want to disrupt Moria's life too much and we hang out at Cat's house all the time as it is."

"Which we need to consider," he said, shaking his head. "Someone might be aware of that routine."

Julia shuddered. "I can't just stop my life in mid-stream."

"True. Okay, I can live with that as long as Adam can help with checking on all of you. Cat knows how to use a weapon. And we'll assign an additional man to watch the school if we haven't figure this out by the time Moria is due back, okay?"

Forcing herself to relax, she said, "Well, we don't have to worry about school for another week, at least. Spring break on the lake—reminds me of high school."

He gave her that tight little smile again. "Cat said y'all used to have some fun times every summer. I wonder how I never got around to knowing you back then. I guess I was away at college part of the time."

"We probably ran in different circles. Cat was older, wiser, smarter, I think. She kept me out of trouble." And he would have been serious trouble, she thought to herself.

"Cat's good at that."

Julia watched as Moria threw pebbles into the water. "Are you sure your Dad's okay with this female invasion?"

"He's just fine. He and Moria have already established a nice bond."

"She doesn't take to everyone. Your dad is a very nice man."

"Thanks. I inherited that trait."

She saw the amusement surfacing in his dark eyes again, and in spite of all the tension surrounding them, she felt a little ray of hope…and a big jolt of awareness. "I think you did."

"So…are *you* okay with all of this?" he asked. "My dad will serve as chaperone and disciplinarian if I get out of hand," he added, nudging her elbow. "Just like high school again is right. And the more I'm around you, the more out of hand I could get."

"You can't flirt with me until this is over," she said as she shifted away. "We agreed on that back at my house when you talked me into this, remember?"

"I don't remember any such agreement. But considering how I got a lecture from my superior about withholding information and going behind his back to investigate a case that was clearly not mine to investigate, I'd say flirting is definitely out of the question right now. But…that'll just make it all the better later, when things are back to normal."

"And will things ever get back to normal?" She had to wonder at that. Lowering her voice so her daughter wouldn't hear, she said, "I mean, I've forgotten what normal *is,* it's been so long since I've felt that way."

He moved closer, the warmth in his eyes glistening right along with the sunset over the water. "I wonder about normal myself. I try to imagine this house full of love and laughter, with a family of my own."

She shook her head. "And yet, you've obviously never married, right?"

"Right." He shrugged, then his eyes turned hazy with

memories. "I've dated a lot, one or two times it looked serious. But…once I got settled into the routine of my job, my personal life kind of fell by the wayside."

"Did you ever have someone special? I mean, really special?"

He looked away. "Once, but that was when I was in college. And it was over before it even got started."

Julia looked out at the water, watching as a dragonfly buzzed over the surface. Maybe he didn't like talking about his personal life. "I loved being married, being a mom. I had it all. Or so I thought."

Eric gave her a measured look. "You seem to be good at the mother part."

Glancing back toward where Moria sat fussing over Rosa, she hoped that was true. "Everything changes when you have a child. Your whole perspective shifts."

He drummed his fingers along the railing. "I certainly understand that. Sometimes I envy my dad. He's had all of that, and even though my mom died a few years back, now he gets to sit back and take it easy, knowing he's a blessed man."

"Or at least he did," she said, "before we were forced on him."

"My dad is tough. He can handle you two. Besides, he has his own place. He can retreat to his cabin anytime he wants."

"I hope so. I don't think he's as thrilled as you seem to be about having us here."

She saw him hesitate before he responded to that. Then all doubt was gone. "My dad always does the right thing. Let's go eat, or he will be mad at all of us."

Later, after Moria had fallen asleep on the couch and they were all three sitting around the spacious paneled den with a perfect view of the lake, Eric wondered if Harlan did resent having Julia here. But then again, his dad hadn't hesitated one bit when he'd called earlier to explain things to him. Eric figured his dad was just trying to protect him, on both a professional and a personal level. His dad sure had seen the ups and downs of Eric's pathetic love life and the ups and downs of being a lawman. And Harlan didn't have to tell Eric that he was in way over his head with this particular work-related project. But they both knew Eric couldn't turn away from Julia now.

Hoping to break the ice between his dad and the woman who was somehow fast becoming an important part of his life, Eric chuckled. "It's been a long time since I brought a girl home to meet my dad, huh, Pops?"

Harlan glanced up from his newspaper. "You can say that again. I thought we were both destined to remain two grumpy old bachelors."

Julia shifted in her spot on the couch. "Let's not get

ahead of ourselves here. I'm not moving in—just spending some time here."

Harlan kept on reading, his bifocals jutting out from his nose. "That's what my Patsy said when we first started dating. Told me she wasn't interested in me, no way, no sir."

Eric winked over at Julia. "Well, I'm sure glad you convinced her to marry you since I wouldn't be here if you hadn't."

Harlan shot his son a deadpan look. "Believe me, I've considered that through the years." Then he looked at Julia. "This one is famous for his hare-brained schemes."

Julia gave Harlan a questioning look, her slanted eyebrows lifting up. "Such as bringing a woman and her child home for dinner?"

Harlan didn't even blink. "Yep. This has got to rank right up there with the time he brought home two baby wood ducks and a bullfrog but forgot to tell his mama they were all cozy in the bottom of his closet. Boy, that caused a regular ruckus around the house."

Julia looked embarrassed until Harlan shot her a grin. "But, honey, you are much prettier than that old bullfrog and a lot less noisy than those scared little ducks, let me tell you."

They all laughed, and Eric breathed a sigh of relief. Leave it to Harlan Butler to get things rolling. "Dad, I appreciate your help on this. I don't think I need a chaperone at my age, but I know you'll make a good one."

Harlan put down his paper, then turned toward them. "I can't say I understand your tactics, son, but I don't cotton to a woman and her child being threatened or harassed. So you both can count on me. Now, let's consider that the end of that particular discussion."

Julia sat up to clutch a throw pillow Eric's mother had cross-stitched years ago with Bless This Mess. "I don't intend to hang around here all the time, Mr. Butler. And while I didn't want to resort to leaving my home, I want to thank you for tonight. I can rest better knowing Moria is in good hands for a little while, at least."

"Call me Harlan," Eric's dad said, pushing up out of his chair, his smile gentle as he looked down on where Moria lay nearby. "Now, I'm old and I'm tired. So I'm going to go across the yard, feed my dog and go to bed. Eric, you'll make sure she gets safely to Cat's, right?"

"Of course," Eric replied, smiling up at his dad. "Get a good night's sleep."

Harlan held a hand up in parting. "Same to you."

After his father had left the room, Eric turned back to Julia. "Finally, we're alone."

She frowned over at him. "Was this your plan all the time, deputy?"

He slid closer to her on the couch. "Maybe."

He watched as her gaze moved from him to the moonlit night. "Hard to imagine that someone could be out there, watching my every move."

"Not so hard to imagine," he reminded her. "I saw

your house today. I'm just glad you weren't there when that man decided to search the place."

She let out a little gasp. "I don't even want to think of that. I just want this to be over."

"Me, too," Eric said as she glanced back at him. "For more reasons than one."

He could see the becoming blush rising up her neck. "No flirting," she reminded him. "For lots of reasons."

"Want to tell me some of those reasons?"

"Not tonight," she said. She got up, pointing toward her sleeping daughter. "It's time to take us back to Cat's."

She moved toward Moria, leaving Eric to wonder what other obstacles he'd have to face once he'd caught the bad guys.

EIGHT

"Ready to go home?"

Julia grabbed her purse off the table at the café, her gaze edging toward Eric. He'd brought her in to see Cat and get something to drink, but now she just wanted to get out of here. She'd spent two hours at the sheriff's office answering questions, and she had gotten the distinct impression that they all thought she had somehow imagined the danger she thought she'd left back in San Antonio. "I am so very ready to go... wherever home is right now."

"I know being questioned was tough," Eric said as she got up, "but at least now we've got everything out in the open. We have your official statement and now we can compare notes with the authorities in San Antonio. This should get things moving."

Cat followed right on their heels. "I sure hope so. Those big city boys were tough on Julia after Alfonso was killed, from what she's told me about their interrogation techniques." After Julia shot her a warning look, she changed tactics. "Anyway, Julia's been through enough. She was nearly exhausted when y'all came in."

"I understand," Eric said, "and I'm sorry it had to be today. But we got everyone together to get things rolling. The sooner we get moving on this, the safer you'll all be."

"If they even believe me," Julia replied, shaking her head. "It does sound farfetched."

"But Tolar's trying to kidnap you and someone breaking into your home was real," Eric reminded her. "And until they prove otherwise, I think there's a connection and I think you're in danger."

Cat patted her big purse. "Well, *I've* got a permit to carry a concealed weapon. And I know how to use it if they come knocking at my door."

Eric lifted his eyebrows. "I just hope Adam *taught* you how to use it."

"Adam, smadam," Cat retorted. "My daddy taught me how to fire a gun a long time ago. I was just out of practice, is all."

Julia shuddered. "I don't like guns. I don't want Moria around them."

"Well, honey, Eric and his daddy have lots of guns out in their cabins." She shot Eric a suspicious look. "Which is why I've been trying to convince Julia all day to just stay in town with me for dinner. I don't see why she has to traipse out to the lake and stay there all day long, every day."

"She's safe spending some time out at the cabin. It throws any watchers off the trail," Eric countered. "And the guns aren't an issue. Dad has all the weapons locked up tight in his office, which is also locked. And I only have my service revolver, which is right with me at all times whether I'm at home or on duty."

Cat nodded. "Uh-huh. I just think you want her all to yourself. I think this is about more than just finding a criminal. You've had dinner with her for two days straight now."

"Cat!" Shocked, Julia headed toward the door. "You are impossible sometimes."

"I call 'em like I see 'em," Cat retorted. "And I don't recall Eric Butler ever being so nice and accommodating before. He usually runs the other way when a woman even smiles at him."

"I'm a very nice person," Eric said, his expression blank. "And this is different—I'm trying to do my job here. And besides, since when are you so worried about my actions?"

"When it involves someone I care about," Cat said, turning off lights and setting up chairs as she moved toward the front doors. "Like I said, Julia's been through enough."

"Don't you trust me to take care of her?" Eric asked.

Cat planted a hand on her hip. "Of course I do. I just don't like you hogging her all the time."

Eric let out a groan. "Fine, then, I'll just have dinner

with all of you at your house tonight. Just to be sure you get equal time."

Julia whirled around. "Cat's right. I've had about all I can take for one day, okay? Cat, we've had this discussion already. I like it out at the lake. Moria can roam around out there. Your place is big and creaky and not exactly childproof, so we can't just stay hidden inside your house all the time."

"My house is not that bad," Cat retorted. "Moria brought half her stuff over there anyway. And she loves exploring my house, especially the turret room."

Julia looked over at Eric. "Moria seems to want to cling to her special things, so I didn't have the heart to tell her no. She brought her doll Rosa and a few other things to decorate her room at Cat's house."

"And she likes to hide things all over the house when she's exploring. She wants me to come and find her and then we have a treasure hunt of sorts," Cat added, laughing. "Which I happen to have the perfect house for, thank you very much."

Julia's gaze locked with Eric's. "I don't like her playing hide-and-seek. It scares me when she won't answer me or come out of hiding when I can't find her."

"You should keep an eye on her even when she's exploring," Eric warned. "That's why the lake is safer. We can all watch her out there, but she still gets some fresh air and sunshine."

"I just want to help, too," Cat said, glaring at Eric.

"People will talk if y'all keep leaving the city limits together at dawn and don't come back until dusk."

"I'm on vacation for a few days," Julia reminded her. "Which is why I came in today to talk to the sheriff. I just want this to be over."

"This is a very small town, honey. Y'all can't keep this a secret much longer."

"We can if no one talks," Eric said, shooting Cat a warning. "And I mean not even you."

"I'm not talking," Cat said, raising a hand. "I know how things work."

"I'll be fine," Julia said. "Right now, I just want to get back to Moria. I'm sure Harlan is tired of babysitting."

"Adam's with them," Eric said to reassure her. "And Cat, if you're so worried, you can call him to bring Moria to town for supper with us." Then he grinned. "We'll be like one big, happy family. I'll even cook."

"I've had your cooking," Cat replied. Then she patted her booted foot on the floor. "But if Adam's willing to bring Moria back, then Julia won't have to go all the way out there tonight—"

"And you'll get to see Adam. Who's working this angle now?" Eric asked, winking at her.

"Adam and I are good friends," Cat said, slinging her purse over her shoulder with a huff. "And since I've cooked all day here, somebody else can certainly provide the meal. As long as it's not you—"

"I'll grill chicken and some vegetables," Eric said as

they walked out the front door. "I do a passable job on the grill. So are you in or not?"

Cat glanced over at Julia. "I guess I'm in. I'd just sit home worrying if y'all leave me all alone."

"Good, we'll have a nice, quiet dinner at your house then."

"I doubt that," Julia said, heading toward Eric's truck. "Not with you two fussing over me." Then she turned as she waited for Cat to lock up. "But…I just want you both to know I appreciate being fussed over." And she appreciated that they both seemed to believe everything she'd told them about her past.

Cat double-checked the door then turned to give them a reluctant smile. "And I want you to know, honey, if I had to handpick the one man I'd trust to guard you with his life, it'd be this man standing right here." Shrugging, she added, "I just had to mess with him a little bit, to make sure he knows I'm keeping my eye on this situation."

"Everyone is well aware of the situation," Eric added. Then he looked up and down the sleepy street. "Except Mickey Jameson at the *Gazette*, of course. We didn't give out the details of this latest incident and we don't want any publicity on Julia's whereabouts, for her own protection."

"Then we'd better get going," Cat said. "You know how that Mickey can smell a story a mile away."

Julia looked around, a chill moving over her like a cold wind. "I agree. His article in the paper after the robbery didn't help at all. Anybody in Texas can find me here now."

"The paper's office is closed up tight," Cat said. "And Mickey's souped-up Mustang isn't in his usual parking spot."

"Good, let's get gone ourselves," Eric said as he opened the door for Julia. Then he nodded to Cat. "Call Adam and tell him our plans."

Julia got inside the big truck, still cold in spite of the warm spring afternoon. She couldn't stop the feeling that even though the streets were deserted, someone was watching her every move.

An hour later, Eric and Adam stood watching the paprika chicken and sliced squash and potatoes sizzling on the gas grill.

"Cat's got a nice place here," Adam said as he looked around the big fenced yard. "Her folks always did take good care of their property."

Eric followed Adam's gaze. The big square yard looked like some sort of secret garden with all its white-lace wrought-iron furniture and the octagon-shaped white gazebo down by the koi pond. "Yep. She's worked hard to maintain this old house and this garden. They don't build 'em like this one anymore."

"One hundred years and counting," Cat said as she came out onto the big cedar deck she'd had built around an ancient pine tree on one side of the yard. "It's a pain to keep up, let me tell you. Always something popping or cracking around here. And the utility bill is outrageous, in spite of all the updates with the heating and air."

"You love it, though," Adam said, grinning over at her.

Eric decided there was more sizzle between these two than on the grill. Adam had been dancing around Cat Murphy for a while now. And it wouldn't take much for him to get all gung-ho about taking things a bit further with her.

Eric prayed his two friends would realize that they'd make a good team. Then he glanced around as the screen door from the kitchen swung open, Moria's laughter echoing out into the yard as she ran down the steps. Julia followed, looking more relaxed now that she'd changed into walking shorts and a button-up blouse.

Watching them laugh and frolic, Eric felt a tug of pleasure inside his heart. They sure made a pretty little picture there amongst the just-blooming clematis running up the porch columns. He wanted to keep them happy and safe. That was his job.

But his heart was telling him to keep them near for other reasons. He liked being around Julia; admired her determination and her need to be independent. And he loved Moria. The child was slowly warming up to him, but she'd really taken a shine to Harlan. Moria and his daddy had taken to walking hand in hand around the trails along the lake. They were good for each other. And Julia was good for him.

He turned back to the smoking meat, flipping the pieces with his tongs. He'd better concentrate on the meal, or they'd be ordering pizza for dinner.

"That smells great," Julia said as she came to stand beside him. Then she looked out over the camellias and azaleas blooming underneath the tall pines. "It's so peaceful back here. Like a retreat. Hard to imagine that there could be anything wrong just beyond this fence line."

Eric put down the tongs, then turned to face her. "Maybe we'll hear something back from San Antonio. They'll reopen the case and go over the files. They could find something to help us."

She pushed at the deck railing. "Or they might come up empty-handed. They never took me seriously when I reported any of my concerns to them before, so why should they believe there is a connection now?"

"Because we do have a connection now. Tolar was here, holding you at gunpoint in front of several witnesses, and now we've matched his gun to the bullet we found in the café wall. He kept saying he had to take you. Then he wound up dead in San Antonio. That's a stretch but it's still a connection."

"But it doesn't mean he's connected to the Gardonez family."

"We'll just have to keep digging until we can find some solid evidence," Eric replied.

She lifted her chin in acceptance. "At least things have been quiet since the break-in."

Eric looked toward the gate to her house, which in the past had been thrown open for Moria to run back and forth. Not anymore. They were more contained with the gate locked. "Why *did* you move into the cottage instead of living here with Cat? She certainly has the room."

Julia shrugged. "It's hard to explain. I love this house and yes, Cat has plenty of space. But…we lived in a huge house in San Antonio—it was very lonely for Moria and me. It just seemed so vast, especially after I started finding things that had been misplaced or rearranged. I know someone had been inside my house. But I could never catch anyone in the act or even begin to prove it to the police."

"So when you moved here, you wanted something more compact?"

"Yes. I wanted a small space, so I could feel secure and in control. That's ironic, since Alfonso always wanted bigger and better. I loved our house, but it was way too big for three people. And after his death, I just couldn't live there anymore. Too many rooms, too many doors and windows and hiding places. I couldn't sleep, couldn't take the tension and the stress. So…the cottage was perfect. We stored our extra things in Cat's attic and took what we needed to move into the cottage. It gave everyone privacy, but we're right over the fence from Cat. Moria can play between her yard and mine. And she has the Ulmers right next door. We walk to church. It's a good environment for her."

"You always put her first, don't you?"

He saw the motherly love glowing in her eyes as she watched her daughter placing chase with Adam and Cat. "Yes, but then, that's what parents do. Some parents, at least."

Wanting to know more, he said, "Meaning?"

"My parents…didn't want me to leave Kentucky. They didn't trust Alfonso. Said he was a smooth talker and a stranger. They expected me to marry a local boy." She glanced down at her shoes. "It always seemed they put their own hopes ahead of what I wanted for myself. And when I met Alfonso, I fell in love and wanted a life with him. They still resent me for it."

"How'd you two meet?"

"He came with a whole team to the community college, looking for people to work in the distribution center De La Noche was building. It meant good jobs for a lot of people, and since I wasn't sure what I wanted to do with my life after college, I applied for a position as a secretary in the front office."

"I take it you got the job."

Her smile was bittersweet, her eyes a shimmering gold green. "I took the job and won over the boss."

"I see," Eric said. But he didn't want to see. It felt odd, thinking of her with someone else. Odd and not very rational. He was fast becoming possessive of this woman. Of course, he reminded himself, that back when she was falling in love with Alfonso, he was falling for another blonde. The one he hadn't been able to save.

Julia tugged at the loose sleeves on her blouse. "Anyway, my parents didn't approve of the relationship. They tried to convince me I was making a huge mistake. But…we got married anyway and I came back to Texas with Alfonso. Since then things have been shaky between my parents and me."

"But they have to care about Moria."

"Oh, they do. They send her gifts on all the right occasions, just as her paternal grandmother in Mexico does. But they're too old to travel and I just can't seem to find the right time to take her there. One day soon, though. I'm hoping I can mend things with them before it's too late. She should know her grandparents."

"That sounds like a good plan," he replied, wishing that for her. "She's a great kid. Dad is in love with her already. She's a nice distraction for him."

"Your father is a very understanding man. I admire the bond you have with him. You two seem so centered, in both your lives and your faith."

He smiled at that. "Our faith *keeps* us centered."

"I need to work in that area, too," she said. "I didn't think faith was a priority in San Antonio. I was too busy living a fast-paced, high-profile life of parties and fundraisers. We went to church, but it was all about being seen with the right people. I wanted to be the perfect wife for my executive husband. I wish I could have helped him somehow. I wish I had turned to God to help all of us."

Eric looked at the woman standing beside him. "I can't see you in that kind of role—the rich society woman. I mean, you seem so down-to-earth."

"I changed to accommodate our lifestyle and now I've changed again since Alfonso's death. I think I've gone through three lifetimes. And now this. I'm tired of changing. I want to be settled and secure."

"I can certainly understand that."

She turned to face him. "Then you can also understand why I'm so hesitant around you."

He had to admire her honesty in this area at least. "You're not ready to take the plunge and get all tangled up in another relationship yet?"

"No, I'm not. I'm still grieving. Not just for my husband, but…I'm grieving the loss of my own naiveté and…my daughter's innocence. It's so hard, knowing that she seems okay on the surface but that deep inside she's hiding some sort of silent pain."

Eric touched a finger to her sleeve. "And so is her mother, I think."

Julia looked up at him then, her eyes shimmering with hope and regret. "I want to be whole again. I want to laugh again, really laugh again." Then she stepped back. "And…I'd like to get to know you better—not just as my bodyguard, but as a friend."

"We'll make it happen," he said, wishing he could kiss her. "I promise."

Adam's voice jarred them out of the moment. "Hey, can you make that chicken cook any faster? I'm starving."

Eric glanced around to find Cat, Moria and Adam all staring at them. "What?"

"You tell me, bro," Adam said, grinning. "I think y'all got more cooking over that grill than just that poor chicken."

Eric checked Julia to see how she'd react to that assumption. After all, she'd opened up to him just a little bit more. Maybe she really did want to get to know him better, as she'd said.

But Julia didn't give anything away, even though Cat and Adam gave them a knowing, questioning look. She blushed a little bit, then shrugged. But she shot him a soft smile before she headed toward her waiting daughter.

Which told Eric her real secrets were still intact.

NINE

Julia woke with a start, her breath coming in shallow gulps. Her heartbeat hit against her temple like a mallet and her skin felt clammy and hot. Had she been dreaming?

Sitting up, she checked the dainty clock on the bedside table: 2:00 a.m. The vast upstairs bedroom of Cat's house was lit by moonlight, the shimmer of the night filtering through the white lace sheers. Hurrying across the hall to check on Moria, she grabbed a lightweight robe and padded barefoot toward the open door between their rooms.

And that's when she noticed the eerie glow in the sky.

Rushing to the window, Julia let out a gasp. The cottage was on fire. Turning to grab the phone, she called 911 then hurried to wake Cat, fear gripping her with a terror that seemed to suck the breath right out of her lungs.

What if she and Moria had been inside that house?

After quickly glancing in on her sleeping daughter, she rushed down the hall toward Cat's bedroom. The door was open, so she hurried in. "Cat, Cat, wake up."

Cat groaned, then rolled over, squinting toward her. "Jul? What's wrong?"

"Fire," Julia said. "The cottage. I've called 911. Get up, Cat!"

Cat rolled out of the bed with a precision that lived up to her name, landing straight up on both feet. "Oh, no. The cottage? But—" She grabbed at Julia. "Mercy-me, somebody set your house on fire?"

"It looks that way," Julia said. "I didn't have much left and this will take care of what I did have. Thank goodness we stored some things over here."

Cat grabbed a pair of pink fuzzy slippers and a chenille robe, then searched for her cell phone. "Let's get down there."

"I'm calling Eric," Julia replied, shock washing over her.

"What about Moria?" Cat asked. "We can't leave her alone."

Julia pulled Cat toward Moria's room. "I'll get her. I'd rather she was with us."

"This will upset her," Cat said as they jogged up the hall.

"I know, but I'm afraid to leave her here," Julia replied. With shaky hands, Julia managed to get on her sleepy daughter's slippers and robe, the scent of burning wood permeating the air as she urged Moria up.

"What's wrong, Mama?" Moria asked on a groggy wail.

"Just a problem, honey. We have to get up now. It's okay. C'mon, Mommy will hold you tight."

Moria didn't protest anymore. She fell into Julia's arms and held on to her neck as Julia and Cat rushed down the long stairway toward the front door.

They could hear the sirens shrilling into the night, but Julia knew it was too late to save her home. The tiny cottage was engulfed in flames. Sparks and ember floated up into the night all around the house. "Oh, Cat, I'm so sorry."

"For what?" Cat huffed as they reached the gate to Julia's yard. "Forget the house. I'm so thankful you and Moria were with me."

Julia looked at her cousin, seeing the bright tears in Cat's eyes. "Me, too." She hugged Moria tight, trying to shield her daughter from the brilliance of the fire. They were helpless against this—the fire, the night, whoever wanted them dead.

Julia needed God's guidance now more than ever. Because she had become so weary, so fearful. How could she go on, she wondered, as she watched the firemen moving about, trying to save her house. Soon the entire neighborhood was awake and outside watching.

Including Mickey Jameson from the *Gazette.* "Ms. Daniels, isn't this your house?" the reporter asked as he came running up to Julia and Cat.

Julia nodded. "This *was* my house, yes."

"What happened?"

Cat stepped between Julia and the reporter. "Mickey, can this wait? We just realized the house was on fire."

"Good thing you were able to get out," Mickey said.

"Yes, good thing," Julia replied, too scared and tired to give the man an exclusive.

"What caused the fire?"

Then they heard tires squealing in Cat's driveway.

"Eric," Cat said, nodding toward her house. "He made it in record time."

Ignoring Mickey, Julia glanced from her burning house back toward Eric's truck. He came running toward them in a long gait, his gaze centered on her. "Are you all right?"

"We're fine," she said, glad to see him. She resisted the urge to fall into his arms. "We're okay."

Eric stared up at the roaring fire. "This has gotten serious."

"So you think it was deliberate, just like I do?" Cat asked, her hands on her hips.

"Very deliberate." He touched a hand to Julia's arm. "Let me take Moria."

She resisted at first, then finally gave her daughter over to him, silent tears falling down her cheeks.

"Did you say this was deliberate?" Mickey asked, moving closer. He snapped a couple of pictures of the burning house, then turned back to Julia. "Ms. Daniels, did someone set fire to your house on purpose?"

"Hey, Mickey, no more questions, okay?" Eric said, nudging the other man to move on. "Not right now."

Moria lifted her head to stare at Eric. "What's wrong, Mr. Eric?" Then she turned toward the cottage, her big eyes going wide. "Mommy, our house is on fire. Mommy?"

"I'm right here, honey," Julia said, wiping at her face. "We're okay. Aunt Cat is right here and we're going to be just fine."

Eric patted Moria's back. "That's right. I won't let anything bad happen to you, Moria, you understand me?"

Moria nodded, her eyes bright. "I don't like bad people. Did bad people do this?"

Eric watched Mickey's inquisitive expression, then shot a look at Julia. "We'll have to figure out what happened, sweetheart. But you don't need to worry. Just rest, okay?" Then he gave Mickey a hard stare. "I said to leave, right now. You'll get the official report whenever the fire chief finds out what happened."

Watching the reporter stalk away, Eric held Moria tight. "It's all gonna be okay, baby."

Moria nodded, then dropped her head against his shoulder. Julia watched as her daughter's tiny arms went around Eric's neck. It was the first time in a very long time that Moria had allowed anyone besides Julia to be that close. She trusted Eric with her bruised little heart.

And now, Julia knew *she* had to trust him, too, and not only with her heart, but with her life.

* * *

"It was arson," Adam said the next morning. "No doubt about that now."

Eric glanced down at the report Adam had just snagged from the fire chief. "Gasoline as an accelerant? Well, that's a stretch."

"Yeah, ain't it though. These people are either very bold or extremely dumb. They've messed up each time they've tried to get at Julia," Adam said, slinging down in the chair across from Eric's desk. "I don't get it."

Eric read over the report. "I think I do. Someone keeps sending underlings to do their dirty work. And so far, they've botched things. And that's got me worried."

"Because?"

"Because sooner or later these people are going to send in a big gun. I just wonder who that will be and how they'll plan to strike."

"We can beef up security around Julia and Moria," Adam said. "I can sleep on the couch on the sun porch at Cat's house."

"I've already offered to do that," Eric replied. "But we could both stay at the house and take shifts. Might make it easier."

"I'm in," Adam said, his dark eyes full of woe. "I mean, this involves Cat, too, now."

"Yeah, especially since Julia has no choice but to live with Cat from now on—or at least until she can find another place."

"When it's safe again," Adam replied.

"Yeah. When it's safe again."

Eric wondered when that time would come. He was even more worried about Julia and Moria now, but not just for safety's sake. This fire had really done a number on Julia. She was quiet at the moment, resigned and watchful, her eyes dark with fatigue. He didn't see how she could continue on with this kind of stress in her life.

Watching her this morning as they'd walked through the ruins of the cottage, he knew she was near the breaking point. It would be just like her to up and leave during the night, simply because she thought she had to put everyone else ahead of herself. And to protect Moria. But leaving wouldn't protect either one of them. It would only put them both in more danger.

"Look," he said, getting up to come around the desk. "I'm taking Julia and Moria to church tonight, to the social supper that kicks off the Wildflower Festival. Maybe that'll at least cheer them up." And give him one more excuse to keep them near. He shrugged, rubbed a hand on the back of his neck. "The house is gone. And we've searched through the rubble. Not much else to do but get the lot cleared. At least Julia had some things stored in Cat's attic."

"Did she agree to go to the kickoff dinner with you?"

Eric slanted his head. "Not at first. I had to do some persuading. She's afraid to leave the house."

"Can you blame her?"

"No, but…we've got a lot of manpower on this now. She's covered from every angle. So…I'm taking her out to get her mind off all of this."

Adam lifted out of his chair. "Yeah, I asked Cat to go with me."

That brought a smile to Eric's lips. "So…you finally took the first step, huh?"

"Yep," Adam said, his expression sheepish. "We had a long talk after the fire the other night. I mean, things like this kind of bring life into perspective."

"They sure do," Eric replied. "I'm liking you and Cat together. I think you'll be just fine."

Adam shrugged. "I hope so. She's as stubborn as a fence post, but she's also cute as a button." Then he turned serious. "Do you think I'm too young for her, Eric?"

Eric let out a long sigh. "Remember that quote by the famous baseball player. 'Age is mind over matter. If you don't mind, it don't matter.' I think that's between Cat and you."

"And God," Adam interjected. "I've sure done my share of praying about it." Then he grinned. "And I've done my share of thinking about Cat, too."

Eric had to smile himself. "Seems to be in the air around here. I can't stop worrying about Julia."

"Oh, you mean—thinking about her in terms that go beyond this case, right?"

"Right," Eric replied. "But I'm not holding out much hope. Julia is in a bad place right now. She doesn't trust anyone, she's still torn up about her husband's death, and she's afraid her daughter is holding some sort of information about the murder. Not to mention, of course, that someone seems to be intent on doing them both in."

"No room in there for you, right?"

"No room at all. And I can't really blame her," Eric said. "But…I'm not gonna give up. I like the woman."

"Same here with Cat," Adam admitted. "I think I've been half in love with her for years now." He tapped his hand against a table. "Just watching her at Nathan's funeral—my heart went out to her. I kind of decided right then and there I'd watch after her."

"That's mighty nice of you," Eric said, slapping Adam on the back. "But in case you haven't noticed, Cat is a pretty independent woman. She can take care of herself."

Adam followed him out into the hallway. "Yeah, and that's the biggest problem between us. She doesn't necessarily take me very seriously."

"You'll just have to keep at her."

"I intend to," Adam said. "Same with you and Julia."

"Yeah, right. We can compare notes later, see how that's working for us."

"Good idea," Adam said. "And in the meantime, I'm gonna stay real close to all of them."

"I'll be right there with you," Eric said, his pledge to protect Julia turning toward a prayer for help from above. "Me, too."

* * *

"I don't feel like going."

Julia looked down at her daughter, her heart breaking all over again. Moria had been through so much loss and pain, she was afraid she was going to lose the child forever. She didn't feel like getting out, either, but Eric had convinced her it might be good for both of them. And Cat had chimed in, saying she wouldn't go to the festival kickoff without them. So now Julia had to convince herself and her daughter. "But…you love going to church. And you know all of your friends will be there. Plus, Mr. Harlan and Eric, too. Even the Ulmers and Fred."

Moria plopped down on her bed, her dark gaze moving over the purple and white swags hanging across the big bay window. "I miss my room at our house. I want my yellow roses back."

Julia sat down on the bed, then ran a hand over Moria's curly hair. "I want all of my things, too, honey. But the fire took everything except some of my dishes and other things we stored here. Did you check the box of goodies Mrs. Ulmer brought over? She went out and bought you a whole set of new books and toys."

Moria bobbed her head. "That was nice of her. I love Miss Nina."

"I love her, too," Julia said, amazed at how gracious everyone had been to them. In a matter of hours, they'd had clothes to wear and all the necessities they'd need to get them through the next few weeks. She was thankful for all of it, but she didn't know how to explain to her daughter that their lives had once again been disrupted. And she didn't know how to convey any hope to Moria.

Glancing around, she spotted Rosa sitting on the dresser. "At least you still have Rosa with you."

Moria got up and grabbed the doll. "Rosa was so scared of that fire."

"I was scared of it, too," Julia admitted. "But we're okay. Aunt Cat loves us and we can live here as long as we need to."

"I like it here, but I miss my bedroom."

"I'm glad you like it. And one day, we'll get back to having our own place."

Julia watched as Moria touched a hand to her other favorite possession. "And you do have the flower that Daddy gave you. I'm so glad you thought to bring that over here with us when we came to stay with Cat."

"I had to," Moria replied. "I promised Daddy. He called it a Texas rose."

Julia's heart burned with that reminder. "Your daddy loved his roses, didn't he?"

"He told me this one would never die, ever," Moria said. "He told me to take care of it and love it, even if it was just silk."

"Daddy wanted you to have beautiful things," Julia said, her frazzled mind too tired to conjure up bitter memories right now. "And he'd want you to have a good time at church tonight. So…will you go with me?"

"I guess," Moria said, her fingers touching the big silk petals of the flower sitting in its sturdy white vase on the vanity table.

Julia watched as Moria ran her fingers over and over the silky yellow material. "How about we plant a yellow rose in Aunt Cat's backyard, as a way to thank her for being so generous to us? And as a way to remember Daddy?"

"Can we?" Moria asked, suddenly excited again. "I know how. Daddy taught me. He said you have to make sure the roots are just right."

"Good, then," Julia said, getting up to straighten her floral dress. "But right now we need to go downstairs and wait for Mr. Eric to pick us up, okay?"

Moria bounced ahead of her, her mood changing from morose to happy again in typical childlike fashion. But Julia had to wonder if her daughter would ever be a typical child.

Help me, God, she prayed. *I need You to protect my child. I don't know who's out there, or why they want to harm me. But Moria is innocent. Please watch over her.*

She reached out to touch the artificial flower Moria so loved. Her daughter had a way of becoming too attached to things. They'd lugged a whole box of stuff over here before the fire, but now Julia was glad they had. At least Moria had those special things to comfort her. Julia thought about one of her own favorite things—

her tea set collection. She'd almost sold it off when they moved, but for some reason she couldn't bear to part with all the dainty teacups and matching pots she'd bought here and there through the years. Maybe because Alfonso always bought her special additions to the collection on her birthday each year. She'd planned on building some shelves in the cottage to display them. But what would happen to her collection now that they didn't have a home of their own? she wondered.

And what would happen if Julia kept spending time with Eric? Would it be the same with him? Would Moria become too attached? Julia didn't want to move too fast, but Eric was a constant, steadying presence in their lives these days. This situation had forced them together. But she had to wonder if in the end, it might also tear them apart. Julia didn't want to become too attached, either.

"I need to go to church," she told herself. "I need to find some sort of peace."

But that wouldn't be easy right now. Because she felt the same as Moria. She wanted her life back. One way or another.

She went downstairs to find Moria and Cat, then heard them out on the big front porch. Glancing through the window, she saw them sitting together in the swing.

Then her cell phone rang inside her purse.

"Hello," she said, watching Cat and Moria as they petted the big neighborhood cat everyone called Prissy.

"Julia, is that you?"

"Mrs. Endicott?"

"Yes, it's me. I'm worried about you. You haven't called me in a while."

Surprised that her mother-in-law was calling out of the blue, Julia stepped away from the open front door. "How are you, Regina?"

"I'm just fine. How's Moria?"

"She's okay. We're…we're doing all right."

"Are you sure? You know I miss both of you so much. I've just had a bad feeling."

Julia didn't know whether she should tell Regina anything about what was going on or not. If she told Alfonso's overprotective mother that they were in serious trouble and fearing for their lives, Regina would certainly fret and worry. But she couldn't keep everything from her. Moria might accidentally let something slip.

"We…did have a scare a couple of nights ago."

"What happened?"

Imagining the petite woman clutching a hand to her chest, Julia took a deep breath. "Our house caught on fire."

"Oh, no. How awful. Are you sure you're okay?"

"Yes…we're fine. We're staying with Cat." That much was true, at least.

"You're blessed to have her right there, and with that big, rambling house, too."

"Yes, we certainly are. So, don't worry. We're going to stay with her until we decide what to do."

"I see. So…indefinitely, then?"

"Uh, yes, just until we can figure something out." Julia had never felt comfortable around Regina Endicott, but she knew Regina loved Moria. "Cat and I are close, and Moria loves her."

"You'll take good care of my granddaughter, won't you?"

"Of course," Julia answered. "So…how are you doing?"

"I have my moments," Regina replied. "I miss my son."

"I miss him, too," Julia said. "It's hard."

"Yes, very hard. A mother's love is so strong."

"Would you like to speak to Moria?"

"Could I?"

Julia went to the front door. "Moria, it's Abuela Regina. Talk to her for a minute before we go to church, okay?"

Moria's eyes lit up as she rushed to take the phone. After she went into an animated discussion about the fire and her new toys, Julia turned to Cat. "Now why would Regina call us?"

Cat shrugged. "She's a grandmother. They call all the time."

"Not this one. We haven't heard from her in months."

"Maybe she's been busy."

"Yeah, maybe."

Julia stared at her daughter, hoping Moria wouldn't give Regina too much information. The last thing Julia needed right now was an overbearing mother-in-law asking her all sorts of questions.

Especially one who'd never approved of her to begin with.

TEN

A quartet was singing an old-fashioned gospel hymn underneath a great live oak while church members and guests strolled around the church grounds. It was a warm night, balmy with a nice breeze, the buzz of mosquitoes humming in the air. The smells of honeysuckle and jasmine mingled with the scent of roasting chicken and sizzling hamburgers.

Julia took a deep breath, embracing the peace that washed over her each time she came to this old church near the lake just on the edge of town. She loved the white, clapboard chapel with the tiny steeple over its big oak double doors. Everyone here tonight was in a festive mood.

She wanted to feel the same, in spite of all the worries crowding her mind. But her conversation with Regina had left her feeling alone and guilty. Maybe she should try to visit Alfonso's mother sometime soon, so Moria could see her grandmother at least. And…Julia told herself, she needed to make peace with her own parents.

If nothing else, she'd learned that time here on earth was very precious and fragile. And so were the people you loved while you were here.

But right now she forced herself to enjoy this nice spring night. Still in shock over the fire and the report that it had been deliberately set, she wondered how she was supposed to pretend everything would be okay. Eric had convinced her that coming here tonight would help put aside any rumors that might be circulating about the fire. But this was a tight-knit community and the front page story in the *Wildflower Gazette* had only added to all the questions and suspicions surrounding her, especially since the headline had read Waitress Involved in Café Robbery Loses Her House to Mysterious Fire. People already thought she'd only brought trouble to this little town. How could she defend herself against the obvious?

Determined to put on a good front for Moria's sake, she asked God to grant her a reprieve against all that had happened to her lately.

"You look pretty," Eric said as he handed her a cup of lemonade.

Julia smiled. "I was actually working on having a moment."

"Want me to leave you alone so you can keep working on it?"

She glanced over at his hopeful expression, something sweet and newborn clutching inside her heart, some strange emotion that made her want to fight for this man. "No, you can be a part of it. Just let me stand here for a minute and pretend that my life isn't falling apart."

She closed her eyes again, imagining his clean-shaven face and his dark, somber eyes. She could smell the sandalwood of his aftershave mixing with the clean scent of his fresh-washed shirt. "I'm thinking that this is a normal night, and we're here to enjoy the kickoff of the Wildflower Festival this weekend. You and I have a date. We'll take a long drive along the wildflower trail, and we'll stop just at dusk to take a stroll through the daisies and red clover. Then we'll sit down on a bench and enjoy the Indian paintbrush and the bluebonnets. You might even kiss me—"

She stopped, opened her eyes, gasping as heat seared up her neck and onto her face. "I'm so sorry."

Eric was watching her with that same warm heat in his eyes. "Sorry for what?" he said, his voice low and gravelly. "I was enjoying that story, a lot. Especially the part where I kiss you."

Julia gulped down her lemonade. "I shouldn't have said all of that out loud."

He leaned close. "And why not? I mean, if you were thinking it—"

She tossed her empty cup into a nearby trash can. "That's just it. I shouldn't even be thinking such things. I shouldn't even be here, trying to celebrate anything. I might be putting everyone here in danger, right along with myself. My house burned to the ground. Someone is after me for a reason I don't even understand. And yet, here I stand, dreaming about a life I'll never be able to have."

"First of all," he replied, lifting a hand in the air, "We've got deputies walking the entire perimeter of the church grounds, and second of all why can't you have that life you just described? Why can't *we* have that life?"

She glanced around, careful to keep Moria in her sights. Seeing that her daughter was at the Go Fishing kiddy booth with Adam and Harlan, she looked back at Eric. "You know why. I can't dream beyond the nightmares I've been having since this all started up. Eric, I'm so grateful that you want to help, but I still think the best thing I can do is leave Wildflower…for good."

He held a hand on her arm. "And let them come after you? I don't think so. If you just try to trust me and listen to me, I think we can end this. Sooner or later, they're going to slip up and we'll figure it out."

"But what if it doesn't work out that way? What if something happens to Moria? Am I a target, or are you just using me for bait?"

"Yes, you are a target," he said, his tone as heated as the brisket roasting on the big grill up near the church. "But we're *trying* to keep you out of danger, not set you up as bait."

"I don't like my daughter being so exposed. We

should be in hiding somewhere, not out here walking around in the open."

"I won't let anything happen to Moria," he said. "Julia, we've been watching Cat's house around the clock, and even the sheriff is in on this now. Anybody would be crazy to try something in a crowd such as this. You have to let us do our jobs. We all believe you."

She shook her head. "I don't know—I've gone back over everything in my mind. None of it makes any sense. I've even tried to do research on my own. I've checked the De La Noche Web site, tried to remember if I stored any of Alfonso's files anywhere, but I can't find anything to help us."

Eric put his hands on her shoulders. "Don't go snooping too much. That could only lead to more trouble."

"Right, so I'm just supposed to sit around, while everyone here tries to protect me. That's not how I operate, Eric. I'll go mad. I just don't know what to do next."

"Well, I do," he said, motioning toward Cat. "C'mon, we're going to take that stroll through the wildflowers so I can convince you that you're safe doing nothing right here with me."

Before Julia could protest, he dragged her past Cat. "Stay with Moria. We're going for a walk."

"Yes, sir," Cat said with a big grin, saluting him.

Julia took a look at her daughter, then followed Eric toward the water's edge. "I don't want to go far."

"We'll be right here," Eric said. "Just try to relax."

She glanced back toward the crowd, making sure she didn't see any strangers. "It's hard, looking over my shoulder all the time. I don't think I've really relaxed since Alfonso was killed."

"Who could blame you?" he said, taking her hand in his. "But we're going to work on that. We're still waiting to see what the authorities in San Antonio find out about Tolar. He has to have some sort of connection to De La Noche, but your friend Luke Roderick isn't cooperating."

She turned to look up at him. "Why are you doing this for me, Eric?"

He looked surprised. "You know why…."

"Yes, you keep saying it's your job. But…you have to admit this is going beyond the call of duty."

"You're a citizen of this county and our town, Julia. And you've been threatened. We have to protect you." He leaned toward her, his dark eyes luminous. "And…I told you, I like you."

She couldn't stop her smile. "You've said that a couple of times."

"Then why don't you believe me?"

She wandered to a bench near the water, then sat down. The wind played through the tall cypress trees, causing their branches to do a lazy dance over the lake. Down in the shallows, two egrets strolled gracefully through the water lilies.

Waiting for Eric to sit down next to her, she said, "I

do believe you. I just don't want you to think there can be much more than friendship between us."

He shook his head. "Even though you were just day-dreaming about kissing me."

"That was a silly dream."

"I don't think it's silly."

Julia didn't know how to tell him everything in her heart. She'd married Alfonso because she loved him. They'd had a beautiful daughter together, but there had been so much left unsettled between them at the time of his death. She wasn't sure she could ever make that kind of intimate commitment again. But when she looked at Eric and saw the goodness there inside his eyes, she wanted to hold out hope that maybe God had brought them together for a reason.

"You're fighting against something besides me, aren't you?" Eric asked.

Julia swallowed back her fear, tentatively reaching toward that trust he hoped to gain. "When Alfonso died, the police…at first, they thought I was a suspect. They found out we'd been going through a very rough time in our marriage."

He lifted his chin a notch. "I see."

"No, you don't see," she said, wondering how to explain, wondering just how much he already knew. "Alfonso was dedicated to his work. He wanted the American dream and he worked hard to get it. His parents weren't very wealthy, but his father was a truck driver for the De La Noche company, so the company helped to give Alfonso a good education. He tried to repay them in every way. Then his father died. After that, Alfonso became depressed and moody. I believe something about work was bothering him, but he refused to talk to me about it. He would pace the floor at night, and he'd leave the house without even kissing me goodbye. Moria was the only light in his life. He loved her so much. Before, when I told you everything, I left that part out. I was ashamed to admit my marriage was failing."

"What happened between you two?"

"We fought a lot. All the time." She looked out at the ducks moving across the lake. "People talked. The rumor was that he was having an affair, and I was jealous. But it wasn't an affair. He was too involved in his job, and in spite of how he treated me before he died, he was an honorable man. Alfonso wouldn't have done that to me."

"But you don't know what was wrong?"

"No. And, honestly, I can't believe anyone within the company would have been doing anything illegal. The family was as honorable as my husband. They still are. They all seemed very distraught when Mr. Endicott passed away and when Alfonso was killed. And to their credit, they stood by me, even when the police doubted me."

"We have to keep digging," he said. "Maybe we're looking at the obvious here. We think it's the family because they've got the power to come after you, and they might have something to hide, but maybe we should focus on someone just outside the family."

Julia looked over at him as a quiet settled between them. "You didn't ask me. You've never once asked me."

"Ask you what?"

"If I killed my husband."

He gave her a smile, but his eyes held disbelief. "Are you trying to tell me something?"

"You're a lawman. You have to wonder. When you first came to see me, to question me about the robbery, I could see it there in your eyes. You didn't quite trust me. Is this why? Did you already know the truth? That I was a suspect in my husband's murder?"

He got up, putting his hands in the pockets of his jeans. "Julia, I know you didn't kill your husband. Is that why you were so afraid to tell me the truth? Did the police back in San Antonio harass you to the point that you can't even trust me?"

"They didn't make my life easy," she replied. "They questioned me over and over. I'm surprised you haven't seen the official reports."

"They don't really want to release all the information to us," he said. "They gave us a very generalized overview and told us that you'd been cleared, but the case was unsolved. They'd chalked it up as a cold case."

"My husband is cold in his grave," she said, the bitterness and helplessness getting the best of her. "That's all I know."

"That and the fact that someone might want you to wind up the same way," he added. "You didn't kill Alfonso, so you can relax if you're worried I might actually think that." Then he turned to stare down at her. "And if you think I'd believe something like that, then you don't know me."

Seeing the anger rising in his eyes, she stood. "I just wanted to tell you that, just in case."

"Just in case it might push me away from you? Is that what you wanted? You thought I'd be disgusted by that information, disgusted enough to…not care?"

Shocked that he'd even think such a thing, she backed away. "You've been asking me to open up to you, to be honest. And the one time I put everything on the line and tell you about one of the worst times of my life, you get angry at me for doing it? Eric, what do you want from me?"

When he didn't answer right away, she turned to go back toward the church. "I have to find Moria."

She heard him stalking after her. "Julia, wait."

But she couldn't face him. She was afraid she'd blurt out the one truth that still haunted her day and night each time she thought about the horrible turn her life had taken.

Had she somehow caused Alfonso's death?

Eric watched the dwindling crowd. Everyone was full of grilled meat, fried catfish and homemade pie and cake. Darkness had fallen over the churchyard and it was time to go home. Glancing around, he searched for Julia and Cat, then saw them sitting at a picnic table with Adam. Moria was playing with some other kids nearby, Harlan right near her.

Feeling sheepish and embarrassed, Eric marched toward them, hoping to salvage the rest of the evening with Julia.

She looked up as he drew near, her eyes full of hurt and sadness. "We were about to leave," she said, glancing toward Cat. "Right, Cat?"

"Uh, yes, right." Cat gave Eric a pointed look. "Unless you want Eric to drive you home."

"No, I don't," Julia said. "And you know something else? I really don't want Eric to stand guard over us tonight. Or you either, Adam. I'm tired of all of this. I want my life back. I'm tired of questioning my own sanity."

Cat lifted her gaze toward Eric, then back to Adam. "Julia, it might not be safe yet."

"It might not ever be safe," Julia retorted. "But I can't expect these two to just move in with us, now, can I?"

Adam grimaced. "What exactly did you two talk about on that long walk?"

Eric stared at Julia. "Not much. We went over the case again. Same old stuff."

"Y'all were supposed to take a night off," Cat said, glaring at him. "Obviously that didn't go over real well."

Adam pushed away from the bench. "Look, people,

this is tough on all of us. But we're a team, here—the four of us. We can't fall apart at the seams now."

Julia started tossing their paper plates in the trash. "We can if Eric thinks every time I turn around I'm trying to distance myself from him." Then she wiped her hands together. "But how could I possibly do that when he won't let me out of his sight. I've gone over all the details as I remember them, but we can't seem to figure out who's after me, can we? We have no leads, we have no clues, and we can't find a connection between my old life and the new one I thought I had. I can't make Eric see that I need some space…and maybe that means I need to get out of Wildflower."

Cat motioned to Adam. "Let's go get Moria. She's with the preacher and Harlan."

"Right." Adam finished clearing the table, then the two of them scurried away.

"I sure know how to break up a party," Eric said, leaning down, his knuckles pressed against the aged wood of the table. Then he focused on Julia. "I'm sorry, all right?"

She put her head in her hands, then took a long breath. "No, I'm the one who should be sorry. I had no right to get so upset with you. I know you're trying your best to help me."

"Yes, I am. And I haven't been completely honest with you, either."

She frowned. "Well, I think it's time we just get it all on the table between us."

"Good idea." He sat down across from her. "You asked me if I'd ever had anyone special in my life. Well, I did, my last year of college. I knew I was coming back here to be a sheriff's deputy and I had this girl in mind to be my wife. But she was torn between another man and me. And she wasn't so sure she wanted the small-town kind of life." He closed his eyes, remembering her beautiful face. "She picked the other man, and he abused her even before they got married. But she refused to leave him. She called me one night, crying, and I went to help her. But it was too late. She died because no one would believe the man she loved could do such things." He lowered his head, his voice going low. "Not even me. I didn't believe her."

Julia expression only mirrored what he felt in his heart, shock and disgust. "But you said you tried to help—"

"I did, that night. But if I'd listened sooner, if I'd tried to reason with her to let me help, she might still be alive." He sat down beside her. "So if I seem overbearing and determined, well, that's why. That's the reason I'm a bulldog at my job. I don't want to ever feel that way again, or to go through that kind of pain again. And that means I'm going to do my best to make sure something like that doesn't happen to you. Got it?"

The color had drained from her face. "Eric, I'm sorry. You should have told me this from the beginning."

"Yeah, well, you should have leveled with me from the beginning, too. But you didn't. Now we're even. But

I had no right to imply that you were deliberately trying to turn me away. I understand that you're scared." He knew he had to be honest with her or she'd bolt like a doe. "And, Julia, I learned from talking to the authorities in San Antonio that you were on the suspect list for your husband's death. Apparently, you were the only suspect for a while there. I should have told you that I already knew. But I don't think that's why you're pushing me away."

She held a hand against her chin. "I wasn't deliberately trying to push you away, honestly. It's just that…I was so ashamed that the police would even think such a horrible thing about me, that I'd even be considered a suspect in my husband's murder. I didn't know how to tell you that. I was afraid you would think it was true, or that the police would gladly tell you that just to harass me a little more."

"Because you tried so hard not to tell me anything to begin with, right?"

"Right. I was honestly surprised you hadn't already found out the truth. I thought maybe you knew and you were just testing me." Then she gave him a direct look. "Were you testing me?"

"I'm not like that, Julia. I wouldn't hold back. I'd want to question you on something like that if I really believed you were capable of doing such a thing. But I don't believe that for a minute. I've seen you with Moria, I've heard you talking about your husband. I know the truth."

She kept her gaze steady on him. "So you weren't suspicious about me? Not even a little bit?"

He had promised her honesty, so now he gave it to her. "At first, yeah. It just didn't add up. But now that I'm slowly getting to the truth, I can see why you'd want to hold back on talking to anyone about this. Especially a deputy sheriff. You don't trust the cops, so why should you trust me?"

She touched a hand to his, the warmth of her slender fingers surging throughout his system. "I do trust you." Then she stood up. "But you have no idea how hard it was for me to admit that."

He took her hand, seeking the connection for just a while longer. "Oh, yes, I do. You said you saw my doubts there in my eyes, remember? Well, I saw something there in you that day Tolar held you at gunpoint. You looked at me, Julia, and I could see all the fear right there in your eyes and it reminded me of all my own shortcomings. But I also saw something else."

Right now he watched as tears formed in those same eyes. "What?" she asked, her tone a whisper.

"You trusted me that day. You wanted to live to be with your little girl, and you turned to me to help you. So, trust me now to make that happen, okay?"

She didn't speak. Instead she stood there looking up at him, a kind of awe shining through her tears. "I'm trying," she said. "And I'm really sorry you lost the woman you loved. But saving me can't bring her back, Eric."

Then she pulled away and rushed toward her daughter. Eric's heart bumped against his ribs as he remembered the agony of knowing he'd failed once. But Julia was wrong about one thing. He didn't intend to lose the woman he loved. He wanted her to look at him and know that she could always trust him—this woman who'd come here to find hope again.

Julia was the woman he loved now.

And still he wondered if she'd ever trust him enough to tell him all the secrets of her heart.

ELEVEN

The next morning Eric's cell phone rang just as he was about to leave the cabin. Answering it as he stepped outside, he saw his daddy walking out to get the paper they both shared.

"Butler," he said into the phone.

The call was from his contact in San Antonio, and after Eric listened to the man's short, concise report, he had no doubt that someone from that city was definitely after Julia Daniels. Turning as Harlan strolled over, he shook his head. "It's like we thought, Pop."

Harlan unfurled the paper, then asked, "How's that?"

"Tolar. He once worked for the De La Noche company."

"You don't say?" Harlan nodded toward his house. "You got a minute or do you need to go?"

"I can take time for another cup of coffee, I reckon."

He followed Harlan back to the tiny porch overlooking the lake. A pot of fresh brewed coffee sat in an old percolator on the table. Harlan poured two cups, used to this morning ritual before Eric headed off to work.

"So…Tolar was connected with the Gardonez family, after all?"

"It looks that way. My source said he worked for them about two years ago. That means he was there right before Alfonso Endicott got killed."

"Think Tolar did the deed?"

Eric ran a hand down his face. "It sure looks that way, but the authorities didn't make the connection during the initial investigation. There's no proof. But why would a low-life like Mingo Tolar kill a high-up executive? I mean, you'd think robbery, but nothing was taken that night. At least, nothing obvious."

Harlan swigged his coffee then set his favorite fishing mug down on the cedar table. "Then you need to look for the not so obvious."

"That's what I told Julia the other night. The family is too obvious and too exposed to pull off something like this. I've even tried to pin it on the son-in-law Luke Roderick, but so far the main man comes up clear as a whistle." He looked out over the dark, calm waters of the lake. "So let's say it was Tolar. Maybe he hoped to rob Endicott and it went wrong."

"Could be. If he was an underling and he needed drug money, I wouldn't put it past him to try something real stupid, same way he tried to take Julia hostage right in front of everyone in that diner."

"The man didn't seem very rational, but not even an idiot like Mingo Tolar would have the nerve to walk into a highly secure, wired building to rob one of its top executives. Unless, like you say, he wasn't there specifically for money."

Harlan lifted his bushy eyebrows. "Bingo. There must have been something else in that accountant's office. Something someone didn't want the world to see." He took another drink of coffee. "Or…maybe somebody sent Tolar to do the job and things went wrong somehow."

Eric thought about that. "That fits with our theory that someone else sent him here. And if that same someone sent him that night, but Tolar failed to get what he went after, then that also fits our theory that they now think Julia has the information—maybe an incriminating file or some sort of bank statement that would expose the company as corrupt?"

"That would make sense," Harlan replied. "But I don't think Tolar would have the sense to know something like that if he saw it."

Eric finished his coffee. "Which means we're right and that someone who is smart is behind all of this."

"There's your connection," Harlan said. "Now all you need to figure out is, what he was after that night and who sent him."

Eric nodded. "And where is that information now?"

He had a bad feeling that these thugs thought Julia

had that information. Or worse, that her little girl had something they needed to find.

"I'd better get into town and pass this on to the sheriff," he said. "Thanks for the coffee, Daddy."

Harlan lifted his cup in salute. "Hey, Eric?"

Eric turned on the steps. "Yessir?"

"How are things between you and the waitress?"

"She has a name, remember. It's Julia."

"I know the woman's name. Just tell me what was going on last night at the church."

His daddy never missed a thing, which had made it hard for Eric to ever lie to his parents growing up. "We had a fight."

"That much was clear."

Wishing this town wasn't so nosy and busy-bodied, Eric shrugged. "We talked it out. This case has all of us nervous. Julia is feeling the brunt of this. She's been held at gunpoint, lost her house to an arsonist, and she's trying to stay sane. It's enough stress to cause anyone to lash out."

"And she lashed out at you?"

"Yes, but only because she's afraid to trust me. The police gave her a hard time after her husband's death."

"Because they went after her?"

"Yeah, they immediately looked toward the surviving spouse. There was trouble in the marriage."

Harlan nodded. "Just be careful, son."

"I'm a big boy, Daddy. I can handle this case."

"I'm not talking about the case. I'm talking about you."

"I know what you're talking about. I'll be just fine."

Harlan looked skeptical. "Then get on with it."

Eric waved a hand. "Try not to catch too many fish."

"Try to catch at least one criminal," Harlan hollered back, used to the teasing.

It was an unspoken rule between him and his father. They didn't talk about the one woman Eric hadn't been able to save. The one woman he'd loved a lot and still grieved.

But that had happened a very long time ago, and just as Julia was reluctant to discuss her past and her marriage, Eric didn't like to talk about the college sweetheart who'd died in his arms one spring night so long ago. Not even Cat or Adam knew that particular story.

But he'd told Julia last night. Not the awful details, but enough to help her see that he couldn't let that happen again. Not to someone he cared about.

Cranking his truck, he sat for a minute with the motor idling, thinking about what had driven him to follow in his father's footsteps. He'd failed at his job once when he was young and inexperienced, but this time things would be different. This time he was older and wiser and he was an officer of the law, not just a kid hoping to become one.

This time he was determined to help Julia and her daughter stay alive. Because he wanted them both in his life for a very long time.

* * *

"So we've determined that Tolar was indeed connected to the Gardonez family," Eric told Julia later that day at Cat's house.

Now that he was back at work, he couldn't use the excuse of bringing her out to the lake each day to protect her. And next week, Moria would have to go back to school. Which meant their time was running out, since the sheriff wasn't too keen on sending an extra man to the school to watch over the little girl.

"I can't believe it," Julia said as she sank down on the back steps of Cat's house. "This means he was sent here for a reason, just as we thought. And that reason had to be that he wanted to take me, to kidnap me. But why? I don't know anything."

Eric took her hand, rubbing his fingers over her knuckles. They were here alone since Adam and Cat had taken Moria to the café with them earlier. The kid was never alone, and that at least was a blessing.

"We think maybe your husband knew something, though. Since whoever killed him didn't take anything, we believe they must have been sent to find one specific thing—a file, or a computer disc of some sort. Something that would contain evidence or incriminating information, maybe. Can you think of anything like that—something your husband would feel the need to protect with his life?"

She blinked, shook her head. "I can't imagine.

Alfonso handled a lot of things for the company. Even though he was listed as head of the accounting department, he did more than just watch over the books. The family trusted him with their most-guarded secrets, everything from food distribution and production to new product placement."

Eric zoomed in on that. "Could there have been some sort of product that the Gardonez family didn't want made public?"

"How would I know?" she snapped, waving her hand in the air. "My husband never talked to me about his work."

Eric let her stew while his mind whirled. "Maybe because he didn't want to put you in harm's way?"

"Oh, so that explains why he insisted our daughter go with him to the office the night he died? None of this makes sense. He wouldn't have put either of us in danger."

"Are you sure?"

She got up, stomped a few feet away to pace in the yard. "I don't know. Alfonso was cold and distant in the months before he died, so, yes, I believe he was hiding something. And I also believe he didn't do it to protect me, more like because he didn't have any choice." She let out a sigh, chased a buzzing mosquito away from her ear. "He was very loyal to the company."

"Maybe too loyal," Eric said. "He took his secrets to the grave." He got up to stop her, putting his hands on her arms. "Someone is trying to silence you, too, Julia."

"Tell me something I don't know," she said, her tone

full of anger and irritation. "It's just that I don't have any more secrets. I've told you everything I can remember."

Eric steadied her, watching as her expression changed from angry to frightened. "But, Eric…Moria *can't* remember. Moria might know exactly what they're trying to find, only she can't remember. Or…she's afraid to tell anyone, even me." She gasped, putting her hands to her mouth. "It's my worst nightmare, what I was so afraid of all along. They aren't targeting me— they want my daughter."

When he didn't try to deny it, she fell into his arms. "They want Moria. And that day, when Tolar kept saying he had to take me—"

"He was probably going to use you to get to Moria," Eric finished, a burning sensation tearing through his gut. "They think she knows something. They don't know either way whether she can remember anything or not. But they're trying to find out. And if she's hiding something…they'll try to look for it or destroy it."

"The fire," she said, her skin going pale. "Oh, Eric."

"The fire and the way they ransacked your house. They won't give up." He held her closer. "We have to prove the connection between Tolar and De La Noche."

"Oh, I think I'm going to be sick—" She pulled away from him and rushed into the house.

Eric heard the slamming of a door as he followed her inside the cool, spacious house. He heard her in the downstairs powder room, sobbing and retching. When she came out, he was ready with a clean wash towel and a glass of water.

He motioned toward a kitchen chair. "Sit here." Then he handed her the water. After she took a sip, he wiped her face then handed her the cloth.

She took another drink, her face pale, her eyes swollen from crying. "I want my child here with me." She grabbed his hand. "Eric, call Cat to bring Moria home, please."

"I will," he said, trying to reassure her. "I will."

Holding her one hand, he punched numbers in his cell to reach Adam. "Bring Moria to Cat's house right now. Her mother is worried." Then he turned away and whispered, "And so am I."

The little group sitting in the comfortable den at the back of the big house was quiet. The mood was somber. Julia couldn't speak, couldn't think past the fact that someone would want to harm an innocent child. But why?

"Do you want some soup?" Cat asked, her voice low and grainy. She'd been just as shocked as Julia after Eric had explained his theory to her and Adam. Even though they'd all suspected this, hearing it with all the circumstantial evidence to back it up made it jarringly real.

"I'm not hungry," Julia replied, her hands together in her lap. She felt so cold, so tired. "It was always there, this fear that they might be after Moria, but now that we're getting closer to the truth, it's so real."

"Why don't you go on to bed?" Eric said, giving her a steady look.

"I can't sleep."

He gave Adam a knowing nod. "I think we should take a little trip to San Antonio, maybe shake up the boys down there."

"Do you think they'll cooperate?" Adam asked, glancing from Cat to Julia.

"Only one way to find out," Adam replied. "I'll talk to Sheriff Whitston first thing in the morning. At least we can go over the files there—see if anything sticks out. Maybe talk to someone in the De La Noche building."

Julia rubbed her hands down her arms. "They won't talk. They didn't want any publicity when Alfonso was murdered. Why would they want to drag it all back out now?"

"They will if we get a warrant to search their records," Adam said.

"Well, now we're at least taking action," Cat said, getting up to stalk around the big, airy room. "I can't stand this sitting around doing nothing. When do we leave?"

"You two aren't going anywhere," Eric said, his eyes on Julia. "Especially not to San Antonio."

Cat made a face. "I probably shouldn't leave the café anyway. Not with all of this going on."

Julia pinned Eric with a pleading look. "Will you assign someone else to watch out for Moria?"

Adam shook his head. "Let me go to San Antonio.

I'll take another deputy with me. We'll find out what we need to know. That way, you can stay here and watch out for Moria."

Eric looked torn. Julia prayed he'd stay without her having to beg. For Moria. Julia might not trust the man with her heart yet, but she did trust him to protect her daughter. Him and no one else right now.

His gaze held hers much in the same way he'd looked at her the day of the robbery. Finally he nodded. "Okay. I'll clear it with the sheriff. You go and I'll stay."

Julia let out the breath she'd been holding. "Thank you, Eric."

Cat motioned to Adam. "Let's go check on Moria. Then I'm turning in. I'm so tired I can't see straight."

Adam followed her. "I guess I get to spend the night out on the sleeping porch again, right?"

"Right," Cat replied. "You're not scared of mosquitoes, are you now?"

"Only the really big ones," he retorted. "I just hope the neighbors don't get the wrong idea about all of this."

"That's why I have the big fence," Cat retorted as they headed up to Moria's room. "Besides, thanks to that nosy Mickey Jameson, everybody in town knows y'all are guarding my house. And since he gave out some of the details, the neighbors know Julia and Moria are in some kind of danger."

"They're speculating about me being in trouble,"

Julia said after the others have left the room. "I still think the best thing I can do is get out of here, go somewhere no one knows me."

Eric dropped his hands on his knees, then frowned. "They'd still find you. These kinds of people don't give up."

"Exactly what kind of people do you think we're dealing with?"

"The worst kind," he replied. "The kind who have something to hide."

In about two minutes Adam came back down the stairs. "Moria is out like a light. Sleeping away in that big frilly bed." He waved his own good-night, then headed to the back of the big house to the screened-in porch where Cat had a sleeper sofa made up for him and Eric to take turns resting. "Eric, wake me up around two and I'll relieve you." Then he whirled at the door. "Oh, and we've got a cruiser patrolling the street every thirty minutes."

"Got it," Eric said, waiting until Adam had closed the door off the side of the kitchen. Then he moved to sit on the couch with Julia. "Want to watch a movie?"

She wanted to fall into his arms and let him make her feel safe again. "No."

He tugged her hand into his. "We have a lead now and a plan, at least. We'll figure this out. We'll keep pounding away at it until we crack this thing. Somebody will remember something, or somebody will slip up. And then we'll nail 'em."

"I hope so."

As if he'd read her thoughts, he tugged her close, cradling her in his arms. "How 'bout we just sit here in the dark?"

"That would be nice."

He didn't speak again. He just held her there until her head was resting on his broad shoulder. Julia closed her eyes and pretended this was a typical springtime night, with mosquitoes buzzing and night birds rustling, a night where the world was sweet with fragrant flowers and with the hope of a love so strong, nothing could break it.

That's the kind of love I can give you.

Julia thought she heard those words coming straight from the Lord to her. And for some reason, they gave her a tiny bit of peace and strength. As worried as she was about Moria's safety, knowing she had Eric and God both on her side gave her a measure of confidence. She couldn't run away; she had to stay and fight for her daughter.

She must have sighed or dozed, she didn't know which. But soon she was curled up against Eric's warm chest. She opened her eyes to find him looking down at her with eyes as dark and dangerous as the night. But she trusted those eyes. It seemed so natural to reach her hand up to touch his face. It seemed so natural to pull his head down to hers and kiss him.

And within that soft, gentle kiss, the world seemed far away and she felt safe and normal and…loved.

Until her daughter's screams coming from upstairs jarred Julia straight up out of Eric's arms and back into the cruel reality of her nightmares.

TWELVE

Julia rushed into Moria's room, followed by three people—all with guns drawn. Eric and Adam quickly did a scan of the tall windows, then checked the closets and the bathroom next door.

"Clear," Eric said. "Let's take a look around outside."

Adam nodded, then followed him out while Cat stood there with her gun aimed toward the ceiling.

"Put that away," Julia whispered as she hugged her daughter close. "It's okay, baby."

Moria sat straight up in bed, clinging to her doll, her eyes bright with tears. "Mommy!"

"I'm here, darling," Julia said as she pulled Moria into her arms again. "It's all right. We're all here."

Moria clung to her, her hands gripping Julia's shoulders. Julia could feel the tiny, erratic beats of her daughter's heart. Pulling Moria around so she wouldn't see Cat's pistol, she tried to soothe her. "Did you have a bad dream?"

"Uh-huh." Moria bobbed her head. "The mean

people were chasing me. They shouted at me. Grandma was crying. And you were trying to help me, Mommy."

Cat came to sit down beside them. "We won't let any mean people get in here, honey. I promise."

Julia wished she could be so sure. Moria had been doing fine until all of the harassment had started up. First thing tomorrow she would make an appointment so they could talk to the therapist in Longview again. Maybe Moria would open up more now. Or the little girl might retreat even further into her nightmares. But Julia knew she had to continue getting the proper help for her daughter.

She pulled back to smile at Moria. "I think we need to talk to that nice lady I took you to see before. The one who works in Longview. Remember when we went and talked to her after we moved here. Would you like to do that again?"

"I don't want to talk to anyone," Moria said, clinging to Rosa. "I don't like mean people."

"None of us do," Cat said, shaking her head. Thankfully, she'd placed the gun on the dresser. "But your mama wants to make you feel better. And sometimes that means you have to talk to another person, so that person can help you to remember things."

"Don't want to remember."

Julia sent Cat a look over Moria's shoulder. "It's okay, honey. We'll figure that out in the morning. Why don't you lie back down now and try to go back to sleep."

"Can I have some juice first?"

Cat stood up. "I'll go down and get some right now."

Julia thanked her, then turned back to Moria. "What happened in your dream?"

Moria's eyes grew big again. "I was running inside Daddy's building. The way I used to run when he and I would play hide-and-seek."

Surprised, Julia pushed curly brown hair away from Moria's forehead. "You and Daddy played hide-and-seek at his office?"

"Uh-huh. Just like at home. Daddy let me hide things, then he'd try to find them."

Julia filed that information away, wondering what else she didn't know about her husband. Apparently, a lot. But right now, she wanted to see if Moria would tell her anything that could help them. "Why were you running in your dream?"

Moria rolled her eyes. "'Cause Daddy was telling me to run, run fast. I couldn't see Daddy, but I could hear them coming down the hall. I hid just like Daddy told me." She shrugged her tiny shoulders. "I tried to find you, Mommy."

Julia's heart stilled. Had her husband had some sort of practice drills with Moria, teaching her how to be safe? Or trying to help his daughter escape in case something bad happened to him?

"And where did you try to hide in your dream?"

"In the bathroom, like Daddy told me. He always said if I got scared to run to the bathroom and hide behind the sofa in there—he said to go to the women's lounge."

"I see. And in your dream, did Daddy give you his cell phone?"

Moria shook her head. "No, Mommy. He only did that in real life. That one time we were playing the game and then he never came back." She grabbed Rosa and hugged her close. "That's why I was scared in my dream. Daddy wasn't there."

"And neither was I," Julia said, a great surging hurt tearing through her body. "I'm sorry, honey. I'm so sorry I wasn't there when the bad people came to see Daddy."

Moria stared up at her with big, dark eyes. "I'm glad you weren't there, Mommy. Or else you might have gone away with Daddy and then I'd be all alone."

Julia sank back on the bed, a gasp leaving her body. Moria was right, so right. If Julia had been on time that night, if she'd gone by Alfonso's office as she'd thought about doing, to pick up Moria, she most likely would have walked in on the murderer.

And she, too, might be dead.

A shudder went through her body as she tugged Moria back into her arms. "You are a very wise little girl. And I want you to remember this—I will never leave you like that again, ever. That's why we're here with Aunt Cat, so you will always have an adult who loves you nearby to help you and protect you. Do you understand?"

Moria nodded. But her next words shattered Julia all the way to her soul. "Because the bad people will find me, won't they? That's why Daddy played hide-and-seek with me. He told me he didn't want the bad men to find me. Only, I think they might find me, anyway. And I'm so scared, Mommy."

Eric turned away from where he'd been standing at Moria's bedroom door, her whispered words twisting his guts into tiny jagged nerves. What kind of nightmares did this child suffer because of something beyond her control? And how could he keep reassuring her mother when he didn't have all the answers and not nearly enough evidence to prove who might be tormenting both of them?

He heard Cat coming up the stairs, then turned to face her. "We didn't find anything outside."

Cat nodded. "Adam told me. He's taking another look."

She went on into the room to give Moria her juice. Eric stayed where he was, but he looked toward Julia to see how she was holding up.

Not too good, from the looks of her. Her features were pale and drawn in the moonlight, the light from the bedside table slanting across her face with an eerie yellow glow. And to think that just a little while ago, she'd looked relaxed and at peace. And she'd kissed him with such a sweet longing that Eric knew he'd never be able to forget her lips on his.

"Everything all right in here?" he asked now, trying to keep his voice even and calm for Moria's sake.

"We're doing okay," Julia said, her smile shaky. "Just a bad dream."

Moria sipped her juice, then handed the cup back to Cat. "Will you leave the light on, Mommy?"

Julia nodded. Eric didn't think she could speak.

Cat pulled back the quilted comforter. "How about I read to you until you get sleepy again?"

Moria looked at Julia. "Will that be okay?"

"That's fine, honey. As long as you promise to try and go back to sleep. You only have a few more days of spring break, remember?"

Moria lay down on the flower-etched pillow, tucking Rosa in beside her. Cat grabbed a book out of the basket Moria had insisted on bringing to her house. "Let's see what happens to the princess. Maybe she winds up rescuing that handsome prince, huh?"

Moria giggled. "Can a princess do that?"

"Of course she can do that," Cat said, her eyes going wide. "Why shouldn't a good, strong woman take care of the world around her? I do believe you are exactly that kind of princess. You can take care of yourself, just like your mama."

Julia kissed Moria, then tugged her covers back around her. "Are you sure you're all right now?"

"I'm better," Moria said. She glanced shyly toward Eric. "You scared the bad people away."

Eric's gaze met Julia's. "We sure did." Then he stepped close, a hand on the floral comforter. "But I think they were only in your dreams, sweetheart. So maybe you scared them away yourself by waking up."

Moria's big eyes searched his face. "I'm afraid to go back to sleep."

Eric heard Julia's sharp intake of breath. He touched a hand to one of Moria's dark curls. "You can sleep, honey. You'll be all right. You know what my mama used to tell me when I had a nightmare? She'd tell me to think of something fun and good right before I'd go to sleep. You know, like going to the beach or riding your bike, maybe fishing out at the lake with Mr. Harlan. Just think about something like that and you'll have good dreams."

Moria looked doubtful, but she bobbed her head. "I'll think about the Wildflower Festival."

"Good idea," Cat said. "Now let's get on with the adventures of our princess."

Eric took that as his cue to leave. "Good night."

Julia walked toward him, her eyes bright. They silently made their way downstairs, then she turned to face him. "Did you see anybody outside?"

"No, nothing. She must have been dreaming."

"Her dreams are beginning to tell me a lot about what happened that night. I think Alfonso had been preparing her for this. I think he knew something could happen, so he wanted Moria to be sure and get away. And she did just that. He got her to safety, at least. But she's remembering that and it's all mixing together—her nightmares and the reality of what actually happened."

"Maybe she'll be able to give us a clue soon," Eric said. "I know we can't push, but she's safe and she seems to trust me more and more, at least. That's a good sign."

Julia took his hand in hers, her eyes warm. "I'm beginning to trust you more, too."

He pulled her close, his forehead touching on hers. "That is a very good sign."

She gave him a peck on the cheek. "I'm still so worried about her, Eric. She seems so fragile at times. And tonight, well, she said something that ripped my heart out. She said she was glad I wasn't there that night. It's as if she knew—"

"But why would he have her there then? If I thought someone was gunning for me, I'd try to keep my family as far away as possible."

She pushed at her hair. "I don't understand that either. I do remember that he had become very possessive over the last few weeks before he died. He wanted Moria near him a lot more than normal. They always had a good relationship, and he was a very involved father. But he seemed to be trying to get in as much time with her as possible. And the way he insisted on picking her up that day." She shrugged. "It's almost as if he'd been waiting for the right time, a time he knew I'd need him to pick her up. I just wish I knew what really happened, what he went through."

"We're going to find out," he told her, lifting her chin with his finger. "I want this over as much as you do. I want you and Moria safe and sound—but my reasons are purely selfish."

She managed a soft smile. "Oh, and why is that?"

He leaned close again. "Because I want you to be able to stop pretending those little happy moments, Julia. I think that's how you cope—you go into a nice, quiet daydream, trying to imagine what life could be like for you and Moria when things are back to normal. And that's what I want for us—normal. Nice and steady and good. And the next time you kiss me, I want it to be real and I want it to be forever. Because this isn't about the woman I lost a long time ago. It's about the one I'm looking at right now. The one I aim to keep…forever."

He could tell he'd shocked her, confused her. Julia didn't like to rush things. And usually neither did he. He was about to kiss her again, in spite of his pledge to make it real when the time was right, but Adam's footsteps in the kitchen pulled them apart.

"See anything?" Eric asked, turning to face his friend.

Adam shook his head. "All's quiet out there. Not even a breeze stirring. Nothing."

"It's too quiet," Eric said. "We'll just have to keep watch."

Adam nodded. "I'll be out on the sun porch if y'all need me."

Eric watched as he left, then he turned back to Julia. "We could take up where we left off before Moria woke up."

"We could," she replied. Then she touched a hand to his face again. "But I think I should go on up and at least try to rest. Plus I want to be nearby in case she wakes up again."

He gave her a reluctant smile. "Probably wise." Then he pulled at her hair. "Try to rest."

"I will," she said, pivoting back toward the stairs. "You should do the same."

Eric nodded, but he doubted he'd find any rest tonight. He was determined to piece all of the puzzles of this bizarre case together, and the sooner the better.

So things between Julia and him could turn from daydreams to reality.

Julia had her own nightmares. Her dreams moved with lightning speed from laughing and happy, with Moria and Alfonso walking toward her along the River-walk in San Antonio, to her standing alone, searching for her daughter amid thousands of wildflowers. In her dream she called out for help. She called Eric's name. She turned but she couldn't find him. And she couldn't find Moria, either. This scenario seemed to loop over and over in her dreams, with the faces changing and shifting all the time. At times she'd be just within reach of Moria, but then Alfonso would appear and tell Moria to run, run. Julia would cry out, but her voice couldn't be heard. Moria would run away from her, and then things would change and the wildflowers would be back, beautiful and lush, and…so frightening because Julia couldn't find her daughter anywhere.

She woke to the morning sunshine streaming into her room and the cell phone on her bedside table jangling for her attention. Bleary-eyed, disoriented and drained, Julia grabbed the annoying phone. "Hello?"

"Julia, it's Regina."

"Uh, hello." Surprised that her mother-in-law had called twice in one week, Julia sat up and tried to stifle a yawn, her mind still reeling from her troubled, dream-filled sleep. "Is everything okay, Regina?"

"Just fine," Regina answered, her laugh brittle. "I just wanted to let you know that I'm packing up right now and I should be leaving within the hour. I'm taking a taxi to the airport and I'll be flying into Dallas."

"Oh, where are you going?"

There was a brief pause, then Regina laughed again. "I'm just so worried about my granddaughter and since we haven't seen each other in such a long time, I've decided to come there for a little visit."

Julia stood up, her heart accelerating, panic lifting the last of her sleepiness away. "You're coming here?"

"Yes, I am," Regina replied. "I've already arranged for a rental car to drive from the airport. I'm coming to Wildflower to spend some time with Moria. I just feel like she needs her *abuela* right now. If all goes as planned with my flight, I should be there late this afternoon."

THIRTEEN

"This should be interesting."

Julia scanned the street outside the café, wondering if Regina would get there before dark. "I don't understand why she decided out of the blue to come now, of all times."

Cat attacked a large enamel baking pan with a steel wool pad, taking out her agitation on the cookware. "Neither, do I. Maybe you should have leveled with her and told her it wasn't so smart to visit right now. Just one more person to worry about."

Julia pivoted away from the pass-through to stare at her cousin. "I imagine you're pretty tired of all of this yourself."

Cat scrubbed away, her yellow gloves covered with grease stains. "Now, don't go getting all guilty on me. I don't mind one bit that you and Moria are living with me. I wanted you to do that in the first place, remember? So just put that notion right out of your head. And if you're worried about my granny's house, the insurance is going to cover that just fine."

Julia put away silverware. "But that won't bring back some of the antique furniture you had in the house."

Cat dropped her scrubbing pad. "Look, I'm just glad you and Moria weren't in that house, so hush up on that. And I don't mind one bit housing your mother-in-law, even if it does seem odd that she'd just pop up."

"You don't know Regina. A complete stranger in your home? Won't that be uncomfortable?"

Cat laughed. "Not really. It's a big house, Julia. We'll put her down the hall from our bedrooms." She wiped her brow across the sleeve of her T-shirt. "Besides, I can see what it's like to own a bed-and-breakfast. You know, everyone thinks I should turn the house into one—just to bring in more people for the Wildflower Festival each spring."

Julia smiled at that. "Well, you're sure getting a dry run. The whole town thinks Eric and Adam have rented rooms and now my mother-in-law." She picked up the tray of dishes she'd been clearing away. "I'm glad she's coming to see Moria but I hope she doesn't upset her. Regina likes to talk about Alfonso and, well, she says things sometimes that make me think she blames me for his death."

"That's silly," Cat said, finishing up on the pans. "Do you think she knows that the police had you listed as a suspect at first?"

"I don't know," Julia replied. "Regina has never been very chatty with me. She saves all her love for Moria, which is fine by me. I just don't need this extra stress right now."

Cat patted her hands dry on a fluffy towel, then started helping Julia refill the sugar containers. "Well, look at it this way. You'll have even more help with Moria."

Julia couldn't argue with that. Moria was surrounded with loving, concerned people here. Julia thanked God for that. Right now, Moria was with Harlan and the Ulmers. Harlan had insisted on taking Moria out to the lake while Julia worked the morning shift, and he'd invited his friends the Ulmers to ride out with him, probably just to keep Julia from worrying too much. Even though Julia knew Moria was in good hands, she'd still been tense and on edge all morning. The sleepless nights were catching up with her, not to mention the constant worry of wondering when these people would strike next. And when she added Regina Endicott to that mix, well, no wonder she was getting a throbbing headache.

"I hope Eric reports back with some news," she told Cat. "Maybe Adam will call from San Antonio soon."

"He might be down there awhile," Cat said. "Adam is nothing if not thorough."

Putting her own problems aside, Julia grinned at Cat. "He seems very thorough when he's around you."

"We…getting closer, yes," Cat retorted, careful to keep her voice low so none of the other workers would hear. "But I'm not ready to jump into another relation-ship with both feet."

"I know what you mean," Julia said. "Same here."

Cat stacked menus on the pass-through ledge. "Funny, how all these weird happenings have brought us all together."

"Misery loves company."

"Or maybe it was just time for both of us to let go of our misery," Cat said. "That is, if we ever get past fearing for our lives."

"Yes, there is that," Julia said, that strange feeling of doom washing over her again. "At least today has been quiet." Her constant prayer for her daughter's safety had helped to settle her nerves, but she kept her worries at bay.

"Looks like the lunch crowd has died down," Cat said, coming around the counter to take a patron's twenty. Smiling at the familiar face, she looked toward the front door. "You spoke too soon. Brace yourself. Here comes Mickey Jameson."

Julia didn't glance up. Mickey was a nice enough man. But he sure liked to badger her about what was going on. She wondered just how much he knew. She wasn't planning on giving him the exclusive details.

"Could I get a to-go of spiced iced tea?" he asked, his smile indulgent. "That is, if you two aren't too busy chasing away would-be criminals."

Cat stared him down. "Nah, today we're back to

being regular people, Mickey. Wish I could say the same for you."

Mickey put a hand to his heart. "Ah, now, Cat, you pain me. A man has to do his job."

Julia tried to ignore him. But Mickey wasn't through with them. "I hear Adam took a trip down to San Antonio. Trying to find some leads, right? But the robber is dead now. What's the point?" He looked right at Julia when he asked this question. "Unless, of course, there is some sort of connection between you having lived in San Antonio, Mrs. Endicott, and that man Mingo Tolar coming here. Care to comment on that?"

Julia turned to face him, a dishrag in her hand. "It's Daniels now, Mrs. Daniels. I took back my maiden name."

Mickey's dark gaze centered on her while he paid Cat for his tea. "And why is that?"

"That is none of your business," Julia said, her smile tight. "I've told you everything you need to know. There's no story here."

"That's not what I'm hearing around town," Mickey replied, moving his straw up and down through the cup lid, the squeaking seesaw sound grinding away on Julia's nerves. "I think there's a very big story here. Only, no one's willing to talk about it. A man holds you at gunpoint, then he gets stabbed all the way across the state in another town. Two sheriff's deputies seem to have become your permanent bodyguards, not to mention your house was ransacked and later burned to the ground. Don't you think the taxpayers have a right to know why armed deputies are watching Cat's house around the clock?"

Julia slapped her dishrag down on the counter. "You just summed it up, didn't you? We don't know who set fire to my house. Cat was kind enough to let me stay with her until I can decide what to do next."

"And kind enough to let Deputies Butler and Dupont hang around at all hours, too. My readers have a right to know if they're in danger."

Then came the reply from a deep voice behind Mickey. "Your readers are safe."

Julia looked up to find Eric standing inside the front door. Letting out a sigh of relief, she nodded toward him. "I don't have anything to say, Mickey. Why don't you talk to Deputy Butler instead."

Mickey laughed. "Good idea."

Eric walked toward them. "I'll be happy to brief you, Mickey. This is a pending case, so I can't divulge the details. However, we're still working on finding out who burned down Julia's house. And right now some of our leads are taking us to other towns to investigate."

"And why are you guarding Mrs. Daniels so heavily?"

"Because she's been threatened twice now. But I can't tell you anything beyond that."

Mickey didn't seem satisfied. "I'll find out the truth, Eric. I always do."

"You're real good at your job," Eric replied. "But then, so am I. Remember that."

Mickey waved a hand as he headed toward the door. "I'll get to the bottom of this story, don't worry."

Julia looked at Eric. "That's what I'm afraid of. If he digs up my past and prints all the sordid details on the front page, I'll have to leave for sure. People will brand me without even knowing the truth."

"He won't get far," Eric said. "But hopefully, Adam will find something to help our case."

Julia hoped so. "No word so far?"

"Nope. But he just got there. Let's give him a day or two." Then as if to reassure her, he added, "By the way, I just called Dad to check on Moria. She's fine. All's quiet at the cabin. We've got diligent neighbors—everyone's on the lookout out there."

Relief washed over Julia. "Thanks for checking on her. She has to go back to school Monday. I'm concerned about that."

"You can always keep her at home."

Cat came by, carrying a tray of salt and pepper shakers. "Yeah, and maybe your mother-in-law can help with babysitting duties."

Eric looked surprised. "Mother-in-law?"

"She called this morning to let me know she's coming for a visit."

"And you didn't try to stop her?"

"Should I have? If I'd told her the truth, she would have

insisted on coming, anyway. She's the worrying kind, and I guess since I told her about the fire, she thought she had to come and see for herself if Moria is okay."

"Do y'all get along?"

"We...tolerate each other," Julia said, wishing she could say differently. "She doted on her son. Now he's gone. Things have been rocky between us since his death. She went to Mexico to get away from her grief, and I have no idea why she's coming here, other than she wants to see Moria."

"Great." He took off his hat and rubbed a hand through his crisp, dark hair. "Just what you needed, right?"

"Right. But I only agreed for Moria's sake. Regina will at least be a happy distraction for her." Julia looked past him out onto the street. "And if I'm not mistaken, she just pulled up. I told her to meet me here."

"You sure you're up for this?"

"No, but it will be a nice surprise for Moria."

At least her daughter would find some comfort in Regina's unexpected visit, whether Julia did or not.

"Grandmama!"

Moria burst up onto the porch at Cat's house, her eyes bright after she spotted Regina sitting in the swing.

"Hello, my little one," Regina said, taking Moria in her arms to give her a long hug. "Sit here beside me. Tell me where you've been all day."

Moria lapsed into a long account of how she'd gone

fishing with Mr. Harlan and her favorite people, the Ulmers, and how Fred, Mrs. Ulmer's little Chihuahua, had barked at the fish and tried to chase turtles.

"It was really fun. I've been out to the lake a lot. I'm on spring break. But I have to go back to school after the weekend."

"My, my, you sure have been busy," Regina replied, her dark eyes sparkling as she scrutinized her grand-daughter. Running a hand over her short, clipped brown hair, she said, "And here I was, so worried about you."

"Why?" Moria asked. "Mr. Eric makes sure no bad people bother me."

Regina gaze quickly moved to Julia. "What is this child talking about? Who is Mr. Eric?"

"He's our bodyguard deputy sheriff friend," Moria said before Julia could explain. "Because of the bad people."

Regina's smile turned into a pinched frown. "What bad people? What on earth are you talking about?"

Moria looked at Julia, her eyes wide. "I'm sorry, Mommy."

Not understanding why Moria felt the need to apologize, Julia nodded. "It's okay, sweetie. Why don't you go and wash up for dinner. You and your *abuela* can have a nice long visit later."

Moria hugged Regina again, then bounced inside the house, the screen door flapping shut behind her.

"What's going on around here?" Regina asked. "You seem so drawn and tense, and now I hear some strange man is your bodyguard. Is my granddaughter in some sort of danger?"

Julia sank back in the white rocking chair across from the swing. "You know about the fire. We think it was deliberate. So Cat let us move in with her. My friend Eric is a deputy sheriff. He's been looking out for us. All of us. It's just a precaution until we can find out more about the arson—"

"I can't believe this." Regina fanned a hand in front of her eyes. "You should have stayed in San Antonio. You had friends there, connections. Moria went to a wonderful school. The Gardonez family would have taken care of you."

"We were lonely there," Julia replied. "I have family here."

"I'm your family," Regina said, her tone bitter. "You could come and stay with me in Mexico."

"I can't do that," Julia said. "I like it here. And eventually I want to take Moria to Kentucky to visit my parents."

"But you could send Moria to visit me for a few weeks. She would be such a comfort to me. Maybe this summer?"

"I don't think so," Julia said, appalled at the thought of Moria being so far away. "She's still working through things…about her father. We need to stick together right now."

Regina rubbed her plump arms with her hands, as if she were cold. "At least you honor her father's memory. I wondered if you'd forget about him completely."

"Why would you think that?" Julia asked, shocked. "You know I loved Alfonso."

Regina's frown creased her olive skin. "I hear things. My son was not happy before his death. I wish someone could explain that to me. I've tried to talk to Luke about it, but he's banned me from the De La Noche building. What did you do to them before you left?"

"I didn't do anything," Julia replied. "I haven't talked to Luke Roderick in months." But she could almost sympathize with the man regarding Regina. The woman always did ask too many personal questions and she was good at making demands. Alfonso had always tried to accommodate his mother's demands and now Regina had no one. Maybe that was why the sudden visit. Wondering why Regina would even want to visit Luke Roderick at his office, Julia said, "I didn't realize you and Luke were so close."

Regina moved the swing back and forth. "We aren't close, but he was good friends with Alfonso and he was very kind to me after both my husband's and my son's deaths. Now he's changed completely. Somebody needs to find out why he's been so distant lately."

"Well, I can't give you any answers about Luke," Julia said, wondering how long she'd have to put up with Regina's disapproval. "But as for the rest, Alfonso and I had our share of problems, but I loved him. And he loved me. I know it's been hard on you. But I'm glad you came to see Moria. She needs a lot of support right now."

"I can see that." Regina relaxed a bit, then added, "But I can also see that you are providing her with a good home and a secure life here. She seems happy in spite of everything."

"She is happy. She still has nightmares, but I've made an appointment with a very good child therapist in a town just west of here. I'm taking her in next week for a follow-up appointment."

"You think my granddaughter is loco?"

"No, I don't think that. But I think she needs some help to sort through her emotions and her memories."

Regina's head shot up. "What do you mean? Has Moria remembered something else from that night?"

"Nothing," Julia assured her, not wishing to discuss the details of her daughter's nightmares. "And she might not ever remember anything. We just don't know what she saw or heard."

"Maybe you're just overreacting."

"Maybe. But she's been through a trauma. That much I do know."

Regina relaxed back in the swing, her eyes on Julia. "And so have you. Did coming here help you any?"

"I'm happy here," Julia admitted. "Or at least I was until we lost our house. I'm feeling a bit unsettled right now."

"All the more reason to let me help," Regina said, getting up to stare down at Julia. "I'll make dinner."

"You don't have to do that."

"It's no problem. You and your cousin work in that café all day. Let me take over for now."

That sounded good to Julia, but she didn't want to get used to Regina being around too much. She wanted her life back. And she didn't want Alfonso's well-meaning mother to stir up things with Moria.

Regina turned at the screen door. "Meantime, think about my offer to take Moria for the summer. It would do my heart so much good."

Julia didn't respond. She couldn't let Moria go back to Mexico with her grandmother. She just couldn't. But she had the sneaking feeling that Regina had come here with that very purpose in mind.

And why now, of all times, had Regina suddenly decided to become so involved in Moria's life?

FOURTEEN

"It's been a few days now, and so far so good."

Eric smiled over at Julia, hoping to convince her that she and Moria would be okay going to the Wildflower Festival on the square in town on Saturday.

Julia looked over her shoulder toward where her house used to be. "A few days can't put that image out of my mind. I just want to keep Moria locked inside." Letting out a sigh, she said, "But I did promise her we'd go. And she's been telling Regina all about the festival. She wants to try all the kiddy rides and the pony rides, too. Do you think it'll be safe?"

Eric didn't want to promise her too much. "I can only say that I'll be close by, and that all the other deputies are well aware of your situation. We're all on high alert, and that includes the police department here in town, too."

She grinned. "You mean the three-man police department?"

"Well, they're still a department, even if they are tiny. And they're just as concerned as the rest of us. We tend to handle big cases by cooperating with each other. Just makes things easier on all of us."

Julia lifted a climbing honeysuckle vine near Cat's gazebo, sniffing its fragrant scent before she spoke again. "I wish we'd hear something from Adam. Maybe we sent him on a wild-goose chase."

"If anyone can get to the bottom of this, it'll be Adam," Eric replied. "He won't back down." Tugging her close, he added, "And neither will I. The festival will be heavily patrolled, anyway, and Moria has been looking forward to it. The odds of someone trying to do anything in such a public venue are very slim. I say we go and spend some time there and try to relax."

"I could use some down time. Regina and Moria are having a great time together, but the woman puts me on edge. It's obvious she doesn't approve of me."

"Is she still trying to convince you to let her take Moria for the summer?"

"Oh, yes. It comes up in just about every conversation. And now, she's got Moria wanting the same thing. I think she's trying to brainwash my daughter."

"I don't think she cares very much for me, either," Eric said. Most of his time spent around Regina Endicott had been strained to say the least. The woman didn't try to hide her hostility or her disdain.

"She doesn't understand why you're always around,"

Julia replied. "I've tried to make her see that you're just watching out for us since the house burned. I haven't gone into detail about all the rest." Then she shook her head. "But you have to admit, you can't keep watch over us indefinitely, Eric."

"I can and I will."

"You had a life before all of this. I'm sure you want to get back to it."

He laughed. "Yeah, I had a life. I fished and I watched ESPN with my dad. And I worked. But this case is big for us, Julia. Wildflower is not used to being caught up in big-city espionage."

"My point exactly. You don't have to guard me all the time. I think when Moria starts back to school, you and Adam can go back to your normal routines. As long as I know she's being looked after, I'll be fine. And since we've already notified the school, and the sheriff has agreed to put a deputy there with the full-time resource officer, I'm hoping Moria will get through this without even realizing she's being guarded at school. I'm taking her to see the therapist next week, so that should help some with her nightmares and maybe give us some answers, I hope. And as for me, I'm usually with Cat all the time anyway. And you've seen her gun."

He grinned at that. "Okay, we'll think about what to do next. You might have a point. Maybe the fire was the end of this. They might think they destroyed whatever they thought you had. But we can't get too complacent. If someone is watching and waiting…well, we just can't slip up now. Not when we've been so careful already."

He saw the shudder moving through her body. She gave him a direct look, her eyes sparkling in the late-afternoon sunshine. "I can't seem to enjoy anything anymore. One minute I tell myself to relax and not worry, but the next I think of what could happen if I let my guard down. At least having you around keeps me sane."

"That's why I'm here. And if I admitted the truth, then I like having an excuse to be around you a lot."

She leaned her head on his shoulder. "Well then, I have to admit I've enjoyed spending time out at the lake and here with you." She looked up at him again. "I can't believe it took my life being threatened and my home being destroyed to make me see what a wonderful man you really are."

"I was working my way around to that," he said, stealing a soft kiss. "I had this elaborate plan to win you over, one way or another."

Her eyes turned luminous. "I wish you could have followed through on *that* plan, instead of having to deal with this constant threat." She closed her eyes. "I'm having a moment. I'm imagining you coming into the café to ask me out on a real date. I'd say no at first, but you'd be very persistent. You'd bring me a cluster of wildflowers and take me to a really sappy movie. Then we'd go back to the lake and sit out on the dock in the moonlight and—"

Eric's heart turned to liquid fire as he watched her sigh with longing. He felt that same longing. "And?"

They heard the back door slam. Julia's eyes flew open and Eric stepped back. Moria came running toward them, her dark eyes bright. And Regina slowly made her way down the steps, a frown on her face as usual.

"I guess your moment is gone for now," he whispered. Then he added, "But hold that thought. Don't let it get away."

"Mama, *Abuela* and I made sugar cookies."

"Did you? May I have one?"

Moria giggled. "Yes, you may. You, too, Mr. Eric."

"That sounds good to me," Eric said, reaching down to pick up Moria. She giggled again, the sound of her little-girl laughter warming Eric's heart.

But when he looked at her disapproving grandmother, a cold chill filled his soul. There was something in Regina Endicott's eyes that put Eric on alert. Telling himself he was being paranoid, he nevertheless decided he'd have to watch that woman very closely.

"I don't think it's wise of you to be flirting so much with that man," Regina said to Julia later that night.

Julia counted to ten for patience. This, too, had been an ongoing thread of conversation since Regina had arrived. "I told you, Eric and I are good friends. I care about him, a lot."

Regina's thin lips were pursed together as she wiped

away at the kitchen counter. Cat had escaped early, since she was on one of the committees to get things set up for the festival. And thankfully Eric was in the den watching an animated video with Moria.

"Are you trying to replace my son so soon?"

Julia whirled to look at Regina, trying with all her heart to understand the woman's frame of mind. "I'm not trying to replace Alfonso. Eric has been a good friend to me and he's helped me through a rough time. He's also helping me to protect Moria. I would think you'd appreciate that, at least."

Regina threw down her dish towel. "Protect her from what? I keep wondering what's really going on around here. No one will tell me the truth."

Julia placed her hands on the counter. "We've had a few scares. For a while now I thought someone might be stalking me. But now things have settled back down and I hope it's over." If she told Regina about her fears for Moria, the woman would go hysterical and scare Moria even more.

Regina's shock was evident. Her olive skin went pale. "Who would be stalking you?"

"I'm not sure. But Alfonso was murdered. We think there might be a connection. I'm trying to keep all of this from Moria, so please don't scare her."

Regina's dark gaze scanned Julia's face. "Do you know something about my son's death?"

"No. I wish I did. I wish I could relax. The best thing

you can do is to continue supporting your granddaughter until we find some answers."

"So that man intends to hang around forever, then?"

"No. As a matter of fact, we had a long talk about that earlier—"

"You mean, when he was trying to kiss you out in the garden?"

Julia didn't hide her anger. "Were you spying on us?"

"You certainly didn't try to hide."

"Look, Regina, I'm a grown woman. I have every right to start dating again."

Regina grabbed a glass from the dish drain, then poured herself some water. "So you admit you are dating this man?"

"We're close, yes."

"Do you think he will be good to Moria?"

"He is good to her. She talks to him and trusts him. She's come a very long way since Alfonso's death. Or at least, she was improving until our lives got turned upside down again."

Regina drank down her water, then washed the glass, her actions full of anger. "You will let her forget her father."

Julia came around the counter. "I tell Moria things about her father every day. She will always remember him, Regina. She was there the night he died, so I'm trying to help her think of all the good times, not that one horrible night."

Regina turned contrite then. "I'm sorry. I know you've both been through a terrible experience. I guess I need to accept that you must move on with your life."

"Yes, you should do that." Julia took a calming breath. "It's taken me months to even begin to think about moving on. I came here for that very reason. I hope you'll try to understand."

Tears formed in Regina's eyes. "I do. It's just that Moria is my only link to my son."

"And you're welcome to visit with her, but don't judge me so harshly," Julia said. "Moria will always come first with me."

Regina lowered her head. "Forgive me." Then she stood back, her spine going straight. "Catherine was telling me she has some old cookbooks stored in the attic. I thought I might look them over and find something new for dinner tomorrow night."

Thrown by how quickly she'd changed the subject, Julia nodded. "Cat and I both have things stored in the attic. I can go up there and look for you."

Regina raised a hand. "No, no. You go on in the den with Moria and Eric. Catherine said they are right by the attic door on a shelf. I'll find them and take them upstairs to my room. I'll pick out what looks good and get the groceries tomorrow."

"Remember we'll be at the festival most of the day," Julia said. "I don't want you to have to cook."

"It won't be a problem. I can come back here early and get started. If we don't eat it tomorrow night, we'll just have it Sunday after church."

Julia was hoping Regina would be leaving Sunday, but that didn't look promising. Her mother-in-law had hinted she might stay a whole week. Sending up a prayer for strength, she watched as Regina slowly walked toward the tiny attic stairs just off the kitchen. "Are you sure you don't want me to go up there for you?"

"I'm fine," Regina said, shooing Julia away. "Go on. I'll be down in a few minutes."

"Well, be careful."

Julia watched to make sure Regina found the light right by the attic door, then turned to go into the den. She could hear Moria giggling and Eric laughing. They were good for each other. Moria seemed to have taken a shine to both Eric and his daddy. And Julia had certainly taken a shine to Eric. But she was afraid to hold out hope for anything permanent. She had to be sure all the nightmares were behind her and Moria before she could give her heart over to Eric completely.

She'd just rounded the hallway and was walking toward the front of the house when a piercing scream sounded through the house.

A scream that was coming from the attic.

Eric's gaze locked with Julia's. He was up and running toward the back of the house in a matter of seconds.

"It's Regina," Julia said, hurrying after him. "She was going up into the attic to look for old cookbooks."

Moria came running, too. "Where's *Abuela?*"

Julia grabbed her daughter. "Let Mr. Eric go, honey."

"I want my grandmother," Moria said, squirming against Julia's jeans.

"Not yet," Julia said. "C'mon." She took Moria by the hand and went into the kitchen, then peeked around the corner. After waiting for what seemed an eternity, she called out, "Eric?"

"It's okay," Eric said, guiding a frightened Regina back down the stairs. "She's all right."

Regina's eyes were wide with fear. "I didn't mean to scare anyone. It's just that—"

"You're all right, aren't you, *Abuela?*" Moria asked, rushing to her grandmother's side.

"I'm fine, just fine," Regina said, her gaze meeting Julia's. "Go up with Eric."

Julia looked confused. "What?"

"Just go," Regina said, hugging Moria close. "I'll be right here with Moria."

Julia did as Regina told her, her gaze locking with Eric's. "What's wrong?"

Eric guided her into the attic, the dim light shining brightly over the jumble of boxes and shelves. "This," he said, pointing to a far corner where the tiny attic window stood open, the white curtains flapping in the wind.

Julia let out a gasp as her gaze traveled from the window to the floor. "My teapot collection."

Every box of her prized teapots and matching cups had been overturned and emptied. And everything was shattered and broken, ruined.

"Oh," she said, reaching for Eric. "Oh, no. What happened?"

Eric shook his head. "Regina said she saw a man in here. She said he left through the window, but when I looked out I didn't find anyone. I alerted the street patrol."

"But how? Who?"

Eric's expression was grim. "Isn't that obvious? Our troubles haven't settled down one bit, Julia."

She put a hand to her mouth. "You mean, in spite of everything, someone managed to get inside this house and do this? But we were here all night. I never heard a thing."

He nodded. "I don't know how they did it, but it looks that way. We had the TV loud, watching that video and we had supper up front in the dining room. But you're right. We would have heard dishes breaking up here." Then he kicked an empty box, his frustration erupting. "Maybe they did the job when we were out of the house and Regina stumbled on them coming back for one more look. It's not over yet."

"It won't ever be over," Julia said, leaning on a wall to stare at the dainty broken floral cups and the shattered teapots. "I've been collecting these since Alfonso and I got married. It wasn't so much that they were valuable.

They just meant a lot to me. Every time we traveled anywhere, I'd buy a new tea set. Alfonso ordered some of them for me on special occasions. I was saving them for Moria."

"I know," Eric said, coming to stand in front of her. "And I'm sorry."

"What now?" she asked, hysteria slowly overtaking her shock. "What now, Eric? We've tried everything. I can't…I just can't keep doing this."

The same defeat she felt shone in his eyes. He was giving up, too. "I don't know," he said, dropping his hands down. "We wait and we hope that Adam figures something out. We just need a tidbit, a connection. We wait and keep trying to nail these people."

"I'm so tired of waiting."

He pulled her into his arms. "I'm not going to stop until we find out who's doing this, Julia. I promised you that, and I intend to keep that promise."

"No," she said, backing away. "No, this is crazy. I'm going to take Moria and I'm going to leave. I'll go some- where where they'll never find me. It's my only hope."

The defeat she'd seen minutes before in his eyes was gone now, to be replaced with a grim determination. "I won't let you do that. I won't. I'll go with you, if I have to. I mean it. If Adam can't give us a good lead, then I'll take both of you away from here until we capture these people."

Julia wanted to believe him, wanted to tell him yes,

he could come with her, but she couldn't ruin his life. "No, Eric. We've done everything. It's time I accept that this isn't going to go away. I don't want to run, but we have to get out of Wildflower. Permanently. And without you."

He tugged her into his arms to kiss her. "I can't let you do that. Not yet. I'll figure something out, okay? I'll figure something out, somehow. I don't want you to go."

Julia didn't want to leave him, but what choice did she have? Someone had destroyed her tea sets on purpose. It was deliberate and it was cruel. But…it could be just the beginning of an even worse cruelty.

Because the next thing they destroyed might be more valuable to her than any kind of collection or possession. The next time, they might finally come after Moria.

FIFTEEN

Eric looked around the attic. "I think we got all of it."

Julia lifted the box of broken china, handing it over to him. "I sold everything I could, but this. Why would someone want to destroy it?"

"They were looking for something," Eric replied. He felt weary down to his bones. This case was baffling, no doubt. The uncertainty of it all was about to get to him, but he wasn't giving up just yet. "Like everything else that's happened, this doesn't make much sense. If someone came into the attic and destroyed your dishes, why would they return to the scene?"

He watched as Julia swept the floor clean to make sure no shards of porcelain were left on the aged hardwood. Leaning against her broom, she said, "Who knows? They didn't get to finish searching the cottage, so they torched it. Now this." Her gaze lifted to Eric. "You don't think they'd set fire to Cat's house, do you?"

Eric didn't want to tell her that his gut was churning

with that very worry. "Not with me here," he said, but he was fast losing confidence in his ability to protect her. Maybe it was time to get her and Moria out of town.

Julia lifted the dustpan over one of the boxes, then dropped the contents on top of the broken dishes inside. "Well, that's the last of that. I'm going to check on Moria and Regina. I think Regina was more shaken than she let on. And I hate that she's now gotten caught up in this mess, too."

Eric watched her stomp across the attic, her shoulders bent in defeat and frustration. After securing the window and making sure the board he'd found to wedge against the glass would hold until he could talk to Cat about fitting new window locks, he left the attic and headed down the stairs to the kitchen. Apparently, the old attic window hadn't been locked at all, since the hinges were rusty and broken away. And someone must have found an easy way into the house simply by climbing up one of the porches and using an old oak limb for leverage to the roof and the attic.

His cell phone buzzed just as he reached the last step.

"It's me, buddy."

"Adam. Please tell me something good."

He heard a long sigh. "I think I might have stumbled on something."

"Talk to me," Eric said, turning to stare across the room to where he and Julia had placed the boxes full of broken china.

"Well, our man Luke Roderick finally agreed to talk with me earlier today. He's clean, Eric. A bit arrogant and he has an ego the size of Dallas, but he's clean. He told me that Alfonso Endicott was a good man, with nothing to hide. He also said that Mingo Tolar had worked for De La Noche at the time of Endicott's death and that yes, the police knew that. But he remembered something he'd never connected before. Tolar had done some yard work for the Endicotts, just to make money on the side. He remembered after I showed him Mingo's picture. An easy oversight, since he wasn't one to keep up with the grunt workers of the company by name or face."

"How would he know that, or suddenly remember it now?"

"He and Alfonso played golf together on a regular basis. That's how Mingo got hired on at De La Noche— Alfonso recommended him for a job on the loading docks. Roderick never met him at the office or at the docks, but when I showed him a picture and told him it was Tolar, he was surprised. He said he remembered seeing Tolar working one day in the Endicott's garden. And it was not long before Alfonso died."

"Then why didn't Julia recognize him?"

Adam grunted. "Because Tolar wasn't working in Alfonso's yard. Roderick saw the man when he went by to visit Alfonso's father during his fight with cancer. Tolar was working for Alfonso's parents."

Eric's indigestion burned all the way to his throat.

"So we have a solid connection between the man who tried to kidnap Julia having worked for both De La Noche and the senior Endicotts. Interesting." Very interesting, considering that Julia's mother-in-law could possibly be able to ID the man. "But the police didn't know about Tolar's moonlighting for the Endicotts?"

"Nah. The old man died right after that visit, and then a year later, Alfonso died. Roderick never made the connection." He huffed a breath. "But now he has a theory."

"Which is?"

"Luke thinks Mingo saw and heard all about the good life of his friend Alfonso—through Alfonso's parents who were proud and braggadocios—and decided to try to cash in on that life by robbing the company. He thinks Tolar had somehow memorized one of the security codes and intended to break into one of the safes but was surprised to find Alfonso at the office that night. He panicked and killed Alfonso."

"Why haven't the police made this connection?"

"They never knew there was a connection, until now. Roderick was willing to tell them exactly what he told me. He easily identified Tolar and suggested he was Endicott's killer."

"So why is this good news?"

"Well, now that I've talked to the folks here and explained that one Mingo Tolar came to Wildflower and held Julia Daniels Endicott at gunpoint, the boys are willing to concede that Tolar probably was the killer. And that should be the end of it, except Tolar is too dead to talk. Now they're wondering who knifed him in that alley. And why. After Roderick left, they had a different theory. They think that someone sent Tolar to rob Endicott and then come after Julia, which means we have bigger fish to fry. And these big-city boys like that angle, since they've been trying to make a connection between the Gardonez family and some illegal activities filtering up from Mexico."

"Drugs or illegal human beings?"

"Neither. They think someone was cooking the books for the family and sending some unclaimed profits to Mexico for safekeeping."

"And Alfonso Endicott just happened to be the CFO."

"Bingo."

Eric rubbed the bridge of his nose. "So you think this all goes back to the family, after all?"

"It sure looks that way. But I don't think it's Luke Roderick. I think it's someone very close to the family, maybe using the company as a front."

"A front for what?" Eric asked, his mind whirling.

"That's the burning question. But the boys here are willing to bring in the feds to help us figure it out. And they're also willing to move Julia and Moria to a safe house until we can prove something."

Eric leaned back against the kitchen counter, a sudden relief washing over him. "I'm thinking that might be our best bet for now." He explained about the attic break-in. "It's just another piece of the puzzle. Ob-

viously, they think Julia has something they need—
something that would expose whoever is behind this.
And I'm thinking Alfonso Endicott was up to his
eyeballs in it and that's why he's dead now."

"I hear that," Adam said. "I'm going to work out the
details here, and then I'll be home. You might want to
warn Julia that she needs to start packing."

"I will. And, Adam, I'm not letting her leave here
without me. You might want to warn the San Antonio
Police Department and the feds about that."

"I don't think—"

"Just do it, Adam."

"Uh…I'll try my best."

Eric was about to stress that he didn't intend to let
Julia out of his sight when he heard her screaming his
name from the top of the stairs.

"Got to go!" he shouted, dropping his phone as he
rushed up the stairs.

Julia stood there, sobbing and wringing her hands.
"She's gone, Eric. I've looked everywhere, but
Moria's gone. And so is Regina. They've both just…
disappeared."

She couldn't stop shaking. Julia tugged at the
chenille blanket Cat had wrapped around her shoulders,
but still she couldn't seem to find a shred of warmth. So
she rocked back and forth on the couch in the den, her
eyes glued to the Amber Alert that was flashing across

the television screen, her mind shouting the words that no mother should ever have to hear.

My child is gone. My child is gone. Dear God, help me. My child is gone.

Eric came to sit down beside her, his hand reaching for hers as all around them officers and officials swarmed like bees, setting up lines and making calls.

Dear God, my child is gone. Please help me.

"Here's what we know," Eric said, his voice husky, his head down, his hand holding hers steady. "Regina's rental car is gone. We're searching for it right now. We have every reason to believe Moria is with her and this is in no way connected to the Tolar case. Julia, we think your mother-in-law kidnapped Moria, maybe thinking it was for her own good, maybe because she wanted to have her granddaughter with her for a while. You have to believe Moria is safe—"

Julia pulled her hand away. "I won't believe that until she's back here with me, Eric." Rocking even harder, she said, "You promised me. I trusted you and you promised—"

She stopped, put her hand to her mouth. The look in his eyes tore through her with a whipping, blistering rawness. She saw the tears misting in his dark eyes, saw the hurt her words had inflicted. "Oh, Eric." She tried to reach for him again, but he shot up off the couch, away from her, away from the truth that stood between them.

Silent and straight-backed, he walked away.

Julia tried to get up, but her legs were too weak. Cat came and fell beside her, taking her into her arms. "It's all right, honey. We're all at our wits' end right now. Things will be better when we have her back." She rocked with Julia, back and forth, as they both cried. "And we will have her back. Adam is on his way here right now to help. And Eric will see to it that she comes back to us."

Julia's gaze slammed into Eric's as he watched them from the kitchen. She'd never felt so alone, so numb. She'd not only lost her daughter; now she'd lost the man she loved, too. It was more than she could bear. Turning away from Cat, she fell against the cushion on the sofa and sobbed into her hands, the nightmares playing over and over in her mind like a silent horror movie.

Eric listened to the radio for any sign that they'd located the rental car. How could an old woman slip right through their fingers like this? How could he have let this happen? He wanted to shout to the heavens in anger, but instead he fell to his knees right there in the middle of the sunporch. And he prayed to God to help him, to find this innocent child and bring her safely back to her mother.

When he felt a hand on his arm, he looked up to find Harlan standing there, his own eyes watery. "Son, are you all right?"

Eric shook his head. "No, Pop, I'm not. I failed—"

"You did everything you could possibly do," Harlan replied, his fingers digging into Eric's shoulder. "Say your prayers, then get up and get back to your job. That's the best way to help them."

Eric knew his daddy was right. He couldn't lose it now. He had to find a way to bring Moria back to her mother. He loved them both so much. And although he felt certain that he'd lost Julia forever, the least he could do was make sure he found the daughter she loved. He owed her that.

So he got up, wiped his eyes and found the strength to put one foot in front of the other so he could get on with his work. "I'm going out to look for them," he told Harlan. "I have to do something, so I'm going out."

Harlan nodded, his eyes full of understanding. "I'll stay here with Julia and Cat. The Ulmers are making sandwiches for all of us. Want something?"

"No." Eric didn't look back as he left the sunporch and headed out to his truck.

If he had looked back, however, he would have seen Julia watching him from her bedroom window. Watching him, and sending a prayer out with him on the wings of her one last hope.

He took the back roads, figuring Regina was smart enough to stay off the interstate. He had no idea why he felt the need to roam the countryside just west of town, but he felt sure the woman was heading for Mexico. And again, something wasn't sitting right with this situation. It just didn't add up. He'd tried so hard to protect Moria from some unseen force, when maybe the danger had been right there in front of his eyes all along. Right there in front of him.

Looking in his rearview mirror, Eric recognized Mickey Jameson's Mustang coming up on his bumper. Mickey started flashing his lights.

Eric pulled over, impatient and ready to tear Mickey's head off, until the other man got in Eric's truck.

"Listen," Mickey said on a quick breath. "I want to help—"

"Then get out of my truck and let me get on with my job."

"Eric, it's the grandmother," Mickey said, his fist hitting a pocket size note pad. "The grandmother is the one who's after Moria. And I have the proof."

Eric's heartbeat hit hard against his ribs. "I'm listening."

"I had a contact in San Antonio who knows how to hack into records—bank records. Regina wrote a check to Tolar two days before he robbed the café. A very big check." He let out a sigh. "And there are a lot more where that one came from, even one written about a week after her son died."

Eric looked over at the reporter. "You'd better be sure."

"As sure as the sun is shining," Mickey replied. "I want to help you find that little girl. Because my gut is telling me her grandmother didn't take her out of love and concern."

Eric nodded. "So is mine."

And then it all came together like a ray of brilliant sunshine hitting across the lake waters.

Regina Endicott.

Regina had known Mingo Tolar. Had hired him to work in her yard. Could she have possibly sent him to find Alfonso that night? Could she have sent him here to find Julia?

And had all of this been an elaborate plan, so that Regina could take her own granddaughter?

He thought about the broken dishes in the attic. Regina could have easily set that up. She'd been alone in the house earlier. Did she go up there searching for something, breaking dishes and throwing things as she went. Had she purposely lied about an intruder?

The window.

Eric remembered how the lock had been open. From the inside. The lock wasn't broken. Or at least it hadn't been, until someone had tampered with it *from the inside*.

Regina had faked the intrusion, because she'd already broken the dishes earlier. Another smokescreen, another piece to this puzzle. But what had the old woman been searching for? Maybe there wasn't anything to find. Maybe she'd just set all of this up to scare Julia, to distract her until the perfect moment. Until she could take Moria.

Eric punched numbers on his cell. He had to talk to Adam one more time.

* * *

Julia heard the call coming over the radio. They'd found the car. She listened, intent on hearing the location. Then before anyone noticed, she slipped down the stairs and hurried to her own car. She had to see with her own eyes if her daughter was safe. She had to know. And she had to confront Regina and ask her why she'd do something so cruel to a mother and her child.

Dressed in jeans and a T-shirt, she started her car and sped off, the sound of Cat calling after her the last thing she heard before she hurried out of town, away from the laughter and the happiness of the festival that was taking place in the square.

Soon, she was on the old two-lane that led west toward Dallas. She knew the crossroads where the car had been located. It wasn't that far out of town.

But when she pulled up, Julia saw Eric standing there, staring at the car, his hands on his hips. He was surrounded by sheriff's deputies and other officials.

She didn't see Moria or Regina anywhere.

Eric heard the car stopping, turned to hear brakes screeching to a halt. "Julia!"

He hurried to her, grabbing her before she could glimpse inside the car. "Julia, you shouldn't be here."

"I have to be here," she said, fighting at him to let her go. "Where's Moria? Where's my daughter? Eric, please."

Eric guided her back, away from the scene of the

wrecked car. Holding her tightly by the shoulders, he looked into her eyes. "Listen to me. Listen. Regina is in the car. She's hurt, but she's alive."

She peered around him, her eyes wild with fear. "And Moria? What about Moria, Eric?"

He pulled her into his arms, holding her head against his chest. "Honey, she's not in there. She's not in the car. We can't find her. We're looking in the woods and along the road, but…we haven't found her yet."

"Hey, Deputy Butler?"

Eric and Julia both looked up as one of the searchers came toward them, holding something in his hand. "Recognize this?"

Eric felt Julia stiffen. It was Rosa, Moria's favorite doll.

He held on, even when Julia collapsed against him, a keening wail shattering her fragile body as the early-morning sun shimmered golden and hot in the eastern sky.

SIXTEEN

Eric pulled Harlan to the side. "We're searched the woods and the road, Pop. We can't find Moria anywhere."

Harlan's wizened face looked haggard and aged. "Do you think she was thrown out of the car?"

"We thought that," Eric said, making sure Julia wasn't nearby. After he'd forced her to come back to the house, Cat had tried to get her to rest. But Julia had been pacing all afternoon, lost in the shock of hearing that her daughter was out there somewhere, either alone or with someone else. So she held Rosa and she paced, and she refused to give the doll over to anyone to analyze or test.

Eric turned back to Harlan. "The passenger-side door was flung open. We don't know what happened, but Regina somehow lost control of the vehicle and it plunged into the ditch. My gut is telling me someone took Moria—maybe it was a planned swap—or maybe not. We won't know until Regina regains consciousness. Adam is at the hospital, waiting for the word to question her." He lowered his voice. "We've called in the search dogs."

He hadn't voiced the possibility of a swap to Julia, but the authorities were certainly looking at that angle. If Regina had help, maybe Moria was safe…for now at least. Unless her own grandmother had thrown her to the wolves. Or worse, unless someone had deliberately taken the child from the unsuspecting grandmother.

His father summed up both scenarios.

"So either Mrs. Endicott passed the child to someone, or possibly someone was following Mrs. Endicott, and maybe forced her off the road and took the child?"

Eric let out a breath. "Yes, and if that's the case, then it's worse than even I imagined. I don't like this. We've got a town full of strangers at this festival and the rest of us are in pure panic mode. I have to go talk to the task force."

Julia saw Eric stalking toward the command center in the kitchen, then watched as he had a long discussion with the other investigators. When Adam walked in, Eric went with him to a corner.

Julia wanted to find out what they were all talking about, but she couldn't seem to move. Eric wasn't keeping her posted right now. He hadn't talked to her on the way home. Instead, he'd just held her hand, as if the strength of his touch could keep her from sinking into the despair that refused to let her go. Did he already know where her daughter was? Was he trying to spare her the very worst?

Eric had been her rock, her link to sanity. And now that she'd lashed out at him, she might lose that link. Wishing she could take back her earlier words to him, wishing she could turn back time and have Moria here in her arms, she thought about what might have prompted Regina to take her child.

She knew Regina loved Moria. But Regina's love could sometimes be smothering and claustrophobic. Hadn't Alfonso expressed that enough when he was alive? And it had gotten worse once Regina had lost her husband. Much worse.

Julia clung to Rosa, the doll's presence a sharp-edged reminder that her daughter was missing. Why had Regina come here? Trying to remember any clue, any tidbit of information, Julia suddenly halted in her pacing, her gaze locking with Eric's across the room. Time seemed to stop, as she remembered that other desperate day when she had searched for him and found him looking at her across the café. Julia tried to relay her need, her panic, to Eric now. And she saw his eyes go wide, saw him step away from Adam.

"Eric?" She heard her own measured whisper, waited as he hurried toward her.

"What is it?"

"I…I remembered something."

Eric guided her to a chair. "Take a breath and tell me what your remembered."

She sank down, her hands shaking as she clutched Rosa to her stomach. "Regina said something the first time she called me—you know—she just called one night, right after the fire."

He nodded. "Go on."

"She mentioned this house. She said something about Moria being able to run around in this big, rambling house."

Grabbing Eric's arm, Julia leaned close. "Only, I never told Regina about Cat's house. I never once mentioned to her that Cat had a big, rambling house. She…she'd never seen this house before. So how could she know about it? How, Eric?"

He looked down at her, his eyes devoid of hurt or anger. "Because I'm afraid Regina is behind this, honey. All of it. She didn't take Moria to protect her."

"What?" Julia blinked, thinking she'd misunderstood. "What do you mean?"

"Julia, your in-laws knew Mingo Tolar. He worked for them, around their house. Luke Roderick confirmed that, after Adam showed him a picture of Tolar. And Luke told Adam that Alfonso had helped Tolar get a job at De La Noche, but Luke never met the man there. He only saw him once, at your in-laws' house. The police think Tolar killed your husband, but we still don't know why."

"But…what about Regina? Why would she be behind all of this? How?"

He looked down, but Julia shook his shoulder. "Eric, tell me the truth!"

Motioning to Adam, Eric waited until Adam came across to them. "We need to tell her everything. Even what Mickey found out."

Julia's pulse raced at a dizzying speed. She could feel the blood rushing through her temples. "Tell me what?"

Adam bent down, then touched a hand to Julia's arm. "Mickey Jameson was trying to get a break on the story, so he got in touch with a source down in San Antonio." He told her about Mickey's discovery. "Regina has been paying Tolar for months now, even though he no longer works for De La Noche nor does any yard work."

Julia couldn't fathom what she was hearing. "Why would she stay in contact with Tolar? She lives in Mexico now. Have you asked her about this?"

Adam shook his head. "She's awake now, but she's not talking."

"I need to see her," Julia said, trying to stand.

"Hold on," Eric said. "There's more."

Adam waited for her to sit back down, then continued. "The authorities in San Antonio think someone at De La Noche was cooking the books. But they could never prove it. Luke got suspicious, then hired an investigator after Alfonso died. They did an internal audit and found some discrepancies. Mr. Roderick thinks that might be why Alfonso was killed. They think your husband either had a part in it, or he knew who did. And they believe the evidence is still out there somewhere."

Julia put a hand to her mouth. "Alfonso wouldn't have done that. He was honest. He was—"

"But what if he didn't have a choice?" Eric asked. "What if he was being coerced by someone very close?"

Julia's head shot up. "His mother?" She stood up, pushing at them. "You think Regina had her own son working to commit accounting fraud?"

Eric nodded. "Not only that, Julia. We think she might have had her own son murdered."

Julia stood in the hallway of the hospital, the numbness that wouldn't go away causing her to hold her breath. Earlier at the house, she'd told Eric and Cat she wanted to be alone, then she'd gone upstairs. After about an hour, she'd managed to come back down and sneak out a side door.

She'd driven to the hospital without anyone even noticing she was gone. She had to see Regina, had to ask the woman what she had done with Moria. And why she might have killed Alfonso.

Now Julia needed to get past the police officer guarding Regina's room. Thinking she'd just tell him the truth, Julia slowly walked toward the private room. "I need to see my mother-in-law."

The young officer looked confused. "Uh, I'm not sure that's such a good idea. I have my orders."

"I know you do, but we're family. I'm worried about her. I need to talk to her."

He glanced away, then Julia heard footsteps coming up the hallway. The young officer looked relieved. "Deputy Butler, this woman wants to see—"

Eric gave Julia a concerned look. "It's okay, Joe. I'll take her in."

Julia let out a breath as Eric pulled her with him to the room. "This is against regulations, Julia."

"I have to talk to her."

"Yeah, well, so do I. Let's just hope I don't lose my badge because I'm letting you go in there with me."

Julia was beyond reason. When Eric opened the big door, she rushed past him to find Regina awake, her eyes full of confusion and fright.

"Where is my daughter?" Julia said, the words coming out through gritted teeth as a cold rage clutched at her heart. She felt Eric's arm on hers, restraining her.

Regina seemed to shrink back, the wires and tubes connected to her body swaying and rattling. "What do you mean? Isn't she back with you?"

"You know she's not," Julia said, shouting the words. "What did you do with my baby?"

Regina began to sob, big tears rolling down her face. "I don't know. We were on that strange road and I got confused. I missed the turn and went into the ditch. She opened the door and ran away."

"What? Moria got away? Are you sure?" For the first time in twenty-four hours, Julia felt a shard of hope piercing her soul. "Where did she go?"

Regina's sobs increased. "I don't know. I…I hit my head. I must have passed out. I don't know. Where is she, Julia? Where is my baby?"

Julia tugged away from Eric's grip. "She is not *your* baby and you will not see her again, ever, do you hear me?"

Eric held her away from the sobbing woman, but she heard him speaking into his radio, issuing an alert. "I repeat, Moria Daniels Endicott left the vehicle on her own. We need to proceed with a search of the entire area surrounding the accident scene."

Julia heard him describing her daughter in official terms. Age, weight, height, hair color, last seen in a pink floral jumper and matching pink tennis shoes. She looked back down at Regina, her rage turning her world red. "You'd better hope they find her, Regina. And while they're looking, you're going to tell me why you had my husband murdered."

It was very late when Julia and Eric returned to Cat's house. Eric knew Adam and the others had gone out on the search, but he couldn't leave Julia. He was afraid she was going to crumble into tiny little bits any minute now, and he wanted to be the one to pick up the pieces when she did so. He had to be here with her. He had to prove to her that he wouldn't leave her, ever. That he loved her, wanted to help her. He wouldn't fail her, even if she thought he already had.

Cat greeted them at the back door, pulling Julia into her arms. "C'mon on, honey. Let's get you something to eat."

Julia moaned, pushed at Cat. "I can't eat."

Harlan stood between the kitchen and the den. "I thought I'd stay here and keep Cat company. The Ulmers are in the den."

Eric nodded. "Thanks, Dad. No word yet?"

"Nothing. They've got the search dogs out there." Harlan looked at Julia. "They're doing everything humanly possible to find her."

Cat guided them into the den where the Ulmers sat watching the television with blank expressions. When Nina saw Julia, she rushed to her, cradling her in her arms. "Poor, poor baby. We love you. We love both of you. We're praying for her. We've got the prayer chain in action, everyone calling around. C'mon and sit here, honey."

Eric watched as Julia allowed Nina to guide her to the sofa. Then he turned to Harlan. "We got a confession out of Regina Endicott."

Cat heard him. "What did she say?"

Eric sank against a leather recliner, exhaustion washing over him. "It's almost impossible to believe." He looked over at Julia, wondering if she could stomach hearing this again. Maybe he needed to hear it himself, just to believe it. "When Regina's husband, Bill Endicott, worked for De La Noche, he made a good living. But Regina wanted more. So in order to please her, Bill started smuggling things in from Mexico. Exotic plants, animals, even humans at one time, according to Regina.

"Then Alfonso joined the company and Regina started in on him. We're not sure how, but he started slowly skimming money off the top and squirreling it away down in a bank in Mexico. But apparently, after his father died, Alfonso wanted to stop. Regina said Alfonso told her there was plenty of money for her to live comfortably, but from now on he was going to control it. But she didn't believe him, and she didn't like not having access to the money. She kept badgering him to keep it up. Then she threatened to tell the Gardonez family and have him fired."

Julia spoke up at last. "She forced her own son to continue the embezzlement. But Alfonso couldn't live with that. He told her he was going to confess to Luke Roderick. Only before he could do that, Regina had him killed."

She started crying, her tears silent and steady.

Eric watched as Nina wrapped an arm around Julia's shoulder, then he finished the story. "Regina claims she sent Mingo Tolar to the office that night just to find a disc. Apparently, Alfonso had some sort of flash disc that he kept with him at all times. Tolar was supposed to get the disc for Regina, so she could find out where the money was located. But he panicked and stabbed Alfonso. He never found the disc."

Julia wiped at her eyes. "And she was there that night, too. That's why Moria kept seeing her grandmother in her dreams. The voices—one of them was Regina. She was there, but thankfully, she didn't know Moria was there. Not until later."

Eric finished. "We think Tolar was blackmailing Regina, but she held him off with the promise of a lot of money."

Julia sat up, grabbing a pillow to hold it tightly to her stomach. "So Regina sent Tolar here to…to take me. I was supposed to tell him where the disc was. Regina thinks because Moria was in the building that night, that Alfonso gave her the disc. That's why Tolar came here and that's why my house was broken into and burned down by another thug she hired. And that's why my daughter is missing right now."

Eric hushed her with a hand on her arm. "Regina paid the second man to kill Tolar and set the house on fire. It was just a distraction to get Julia and Moria out of the house. But the man panicked and can't be found. So she came here herself, hoping to find the flash disc. She broke the dishes in the attic, hoping to scare Julia into coming to Mexico with her—or at least letting her take Moria."

"So she could harass Moria until…until she remembered," Julia said, gulping back a breath. She pushed away from the couch. "I…I need to…to find my daughter. Eric, I have to find her."

Eric pulled Julia into his arms, his heart breaking with each sob he felt shuddering through her shoulders. "We'll find her. I promise."

But he was fast running out of promises.

Then he heard the back door open, and Adam came bursting into the room. "The dogs, Eric. The dogs tracked Moria's scent back to this house. We think Moria might be hiding somewhere in here."

Cat jumped up and ran into Adam's arms. "Oh, bless you."

Then Eric started bobbing his head. "You're right. She plays hide-and-seek. That's her game. And she hides things all over the house, right?" He looked over at Julia. "Think about it. If Alfonso coached Moria to hide the disc and to hide herself, then she's probably been right under our noses since she left that car. Julia, she might be right here, playing hide-and-seek, waiting for us to find her."

Julia sank against Eric's chest, tears of joy washing over her. "We have to look for her." Then she turned to Adam. "We can't bring the dogs in here. They'll scare her. Just…give me a few minutes by myself to try and find her, okay?"

"C'mon," Eric said, "we'll look together." Then he stared down at Julia. "But where do you think we should start?"

Julia sent up a prayer, afraid to hope. "She loves the turret room."

Julia looked in Moria's room, trying to imagine where her daughter might try to hide, her prayers as steady as the beat of her heart coursing through her body. Glancing around, she immediately stopped when her gaze moved over the old vanity. "Eric, her yellow rose is missing."

"What rose?" Eric asked, right behind her.

"The one Alfonso gave her. It was a huge, silk thing on a heavy stem in a pot with fake grass. She loved that flower. She brought it over here when we left the cottage."

"You think she has it with her?"

Julia nodded. "She dropped Rosa in the grass by the car for some reason. And she never lets go of Rosa. Next to the doll, that silk flower was her favorite possession."

"Maybe she has it with her now," he said. "Let's keep looking."

Julia softly called Moria's name. "Moria, honey, are you here? Please answer Mommy."

As they made their way through all the second-floor bedrooms, Julia shuddered when they neared the one Regina had stayed in. "This one is right near the turret room," she whispered. "But I don't think Moria would go in there, especially if Regina threatened her or scared her."

"Okay. We'll have to send the team in here anyway to see if Regina left anything for us," Eric said. "Let's try the turret room first."

Julia started up the narrow spiral stairs to the octagon shaped turret room at the top of the old house. "Moria, it's Mommy. Please answer me. This isn't a game, honey. We need you to come out."

At first they heard nothing. Then there was a slight shifting sound coming from inside the tiny room.

"Moria, it's Mr. Eric. You're safe now. You don't have to hide anymore. And you don't have to hide anything that your daddy gave you, either. The bad men won't be coming back."

Julia pushed at the tiny door, then slowly opened it, willing herself to stay calm, no matter what they found. And inside, sitting by the window box with her yellow silk rose clutched in her hands, was her daughter.

Later that night, after the officials had taken statements and after the neighbors and well-wishers had left, Julia stood out on the back porch, breathing in the sweet scents of honeysuckle and clover. Off in the distance, she could hear the celebration at the Wildflower Festival.

Now the town had a real reason to celebrate. Moria was safe, at last. The sheriff had announced it on the loud-speaker immediately after they'd rushed downstairs with Moria clinging to Eric's neck. And all the people who'd been holding vigils now were laughing and rejoicing.

Moria was safe. Julia let those words echo in her mind over and over. A doctor had checked her out and proclaimed her to be physically fit. Her trek back up the road to town had brought her a few scrapes and bug bites, but she was fine. She had somehow known to run—run toward her family, run toward home.

Emotionally, though, Julia knew her daughter was still suffering. How did you explain to a little girl that her grandmother had gone off the deep end because of greed and grief and money? It would take months of therapy to make sure Moria had no more nightmares in her life.

And Regina would be spending a lot of time behind bars, thinking about what her greed had done to her family. Moria had shown them the tiny little flash disc, hidden safely in the bottom of the florist moss covering her beloved yellow rose. The rose her father had given her, telling her to keep it with her always. Moria hadn't even know the disc was there until she'd sat hidden and afraid in the tiny room, waiting for someone to come and find her.

Julia understood it all now. Alfonso had been afraid Regina would try to take Moria in order to blackmail him into cooperating. He was trying to protect his child by bringing her to work with him, by keeping her close. Just as Julia had tried to protect her since his death. How he must have suffered, all alone and afraid, and too ashamed and embarrassed to tell even his wife.

I didn't love him enough, Julia thought now. *I didn't help him enough.* She silently asked God to give her a second chance to really, truly love. To love God and to love Eric.

Then she heard the screen door creaking open and turned to find Eric walking toward her, his dark eyes glinting in the muted yard light.

"Hi," he said.

"Hi." She closed her eyes, hoping she could tell him everything inside her heart. "Eric, I'm sorry—"

He pulled her close, wrapping his arms around her waist as he leaned his head on top of hers. "It's over. All of it. Time for a fresh start. Time for that date I wanted to take you on."

She smiled, her eyes still closed. "I'm having a moment."

"Are you? And what's happening in your moment?"

Snuggling back against his strong body, she said, "It's spring and the wildflowers are blooming out by the lake. You and I are walking along, holding hands. Moria is running in front of us, chasing a butterfly. We're safe, we're happy—"

He turned her in his arms. "And I'm kissing you, right?"

She opened her eyes. "Right."

His lips touched hers, warm and solid and endearingly sweet. Then he lifted his head and looked down at her. "You know, I'm having a moment of my own."

"Really?"

"Uh-huh. I can see you dressed in something frilly and pretty, walking up the church aisle toward me.

You're smiling. And Moria is your flower girl. She's carrying a basket of bluebonnets and black-eyed Susans. The church is packed and I'm waiting to take my wedding vows. I'm waiting to make you my wife."

Julia sighed, touched a hand to his face. "I like that moment."

"How 'bout we make it a lifetime, instead of just a moment?"

"I like that even better."

"You're safe here with me, Julia."

"I know that now."

He held her there in the moonlight, and as she looked over his shoulder and out into the night, she could see the wildflowers dancing in the grass, dancing as part of God's celebration. And as part of His promise of a love so strong, nothing could break it.

* * * * *

Dear Reader:

We all have secret places where we hide things. Maybe it's our jewelry or money, or we might keep a secret for someone close. That is what little Moria was trying to do in this story. She loved her father and tried to do as he'd asked by hiding something very important. That strong love and her need to remember her father caused this child to have nightmares. It also put her in danger.

Eric and Julia both wanted to protect Moria, but the answers were hard for them to accept. It's always hard when someone we love and trust betrays us. Julia couldn't trust Eric because she felt betrayed by her husband's secrets, and that betrayal endangered her child. We sometimes might feel this way about trusting God, but if we give our secrets and our fears over to Him, we will find peace.

I'd love to hear from you. Visit my website at www.lenoraworth.com!

Until next time, may the angels watch over you, always.

Lenora Worth

QUESTIONS FOR DISCUSSION

1. Why did Julia insist on keeping her past a secret?

2. What did Eric do to gain Julia's trust? Why do you think it's hard to trust others at times?

3. Why did Moria keep what her daddy had given her a secret? Do you think Alfonzo was wrong to ask this of his young daughter?

4. What motivated Julia's mother-in-law to do what she did? What would you have done in her situation?

5. How does greed cause us to lose sight of our faith? Has this ever happened to you or someone you know?

6. Eric was an honorable man, but he had a soft spot for Julia and Moria. Do you think this clouded his judgment?

7. How did Eric help Julia find her faith again? Do you think small-town living is better than the big city? Why or why not?

8. What kind of relationship did Eric have with his father? Do you wish you could be closer to those you love?

9. Did Julia do the right thing, moving away from San Antonio? Do you think she was safe in Wildflower? Why or why not?

10. How can we reveal the secret things we're hiding? Should we turn to God and tell Him first? What secrets would you like to let go of in your own life?

"Welcome to the family, Briton," said one of Olaf's men in a mocking voice. "We look forward to the presence of a woman at our hall."

Bronwen grasped her tunic and yanked it from the Viking's thick fingers. As she stepped away from the table, she heard the drunken laughter of the barbarians behind her. How could her father have betrothed her to the old Viking?

Running down the steps toward the heavy oak door that led outside the keep, Bronwen gathered her mantle about her. She ordered the doorman to open it, and he did so reluctantly, pressing her to carry a torch. But Bronwen pushed past him and fled into the darkness.

Dashing down the steep, pebbled hill toward the beach, she felt the frozen ground give way to sand. She threw off her veil and circlet and kicked away her shoes.

Racing alongside the pounding surf, she felt hot tears of anger and shame well up and stream down her cheeks. With no concern for her safety, Bronwen ran and ran, her long braids streaming behind her, falling loose, drifting like a tattered black flag.

Blinded with weeping, she did not see the dark form that loomed suddenly in her path and stopped dead her headlong sprint. Bronwen shrieked in surprise and fear as iron arms pinned her, and a heavy cloak threatened to suffocate her.

"Release me!" she cried. "Guard! Guard, help me!"

"Hush, my lady." A deep voice emanated from the darkness. "I mean you no harm. What demon drives you to run so madly in the night without fear for your safety?"

"Release me, villain! I am the daughter—"

"I shall hold you until you calm yourself. We had heard there were witches in Amounderness, but I had not thought to meet one so openly."

Still held tight in the man's arms, Bronwen drew back and peered up at the hooded figure. "You! You are the man who spied on our feast. Release me at once, or I shall call the guard upon you."

The man chuckled at this and turned toward his companions, who stood in a group nearby. Bronwen caught hold of the back of his hood and jerked it down to reveal a head of glossy raven curls. But the man's face was shrouded in darkness yet, and as he looked at her, she could not read his expression.

"So you are the blessed bride-to-be." He pulled the hood back over his head. "Your father has paired you with an interesting choice."

Relieved that her captor did not appear to be a high-wayman, she sagged from his warm hands onto the wet sand. "Please leave me here alone. I need peace to think. Go on your way."

The tall stranger shrugged off his outer mantle and wrapped it around her shoulders. "Why did your father betroth you thus to the aged Viking?" he asked.

"For one purported to be a spy, you know precious little about Amounderness. But I shall tell you, as it is all common knowledge."

She pulled the cloak tightly about her, reveling in its warmth. "Our land, Amounderness, once was Briton territory. Olaf Lothbrok, my betrothed, came here as a youth when the Viking invasions had nearly subsided. He took the lands directly to the south of Rossall Hall from their Briton lord. Then, of course, the Normans came, and Amounderness was pillaged by William the Conqueror's army."

The man squatted on the sand beside Bronwen. He listened with obvious interest as she continued the familiar tale. "When William took an account of Amounderness in his Domesday Book, he recorded no remaining lords and few people at all. But he did not know the Britons. Slowly we crept out of hiding and returned to our halls. My father's family reoccupied Rossall Hall. And there we live, as we should, watching over our serfs as they fish and grow their meager crops. Indeed, there is not much here for the greedy Normans to want, if they are the ones for whom you spy."

Unwilling to continue speaking when her heart was so heavy, Bronwen stood and turned toward the sea. The traveler rose beside her and touched her arm. "Olaf Lothbrok's lands—together with your father's—will reunite most of Amounderness. A clever plan. You sister's future husband holds the rest of the adjoining lands, I understand."

"You've done your work, sir. Your lord will be pleased. Who is he—some land-hungry Scottish baron? Or have you forgotten that King Stephen gave Amounderness to the Scots as a trade for their support in his war with Matilda? I certainly hope your lord is not a Norman. He would be so disappointed to learn he has no legal rights here. Now, if you will excuse me?"

Bronwen turned and began walking back along the beach toward Rosall Hall. She felt better for her run, and somehow her father's plan did not seem so far-fetched anymore. Distant lights twinkled through the fog that was rolling in from the west, and she suddenly realized what a long way she had come.

"My lady," the stranger's voice called out behind her.

Bronwen kept walking, unwilling to face again the one who had seen her in her humiliation. She did not care what he reported to his master.

"My lady, you have a bit of a walk ahead of you." The

traveler strode forward to join her. "Perhaps I should accompany you to your destination."

"You leave me no choice, I see."

"I am not one to compromise myself, dear lady. I follow the path God has set before me and none other."

"And just who are you?"

"I am called Jacques."

"French. A Norman, as I had suspected."

The man chuckled. "Not nearly as Norman as you are Briton."

As they approached the fortress, Bronwen could see that the guests had not yet begun to disperse. Perhaps no one had missed her, and she could slip quietly into bed beside Gildan.

She turned to go, but he took her arm and studied her face in the moonlight. Then, gently, he drew her into the folds of his hooded cloak. "Perhaps the bride would like the memory of a younger man's embrace to warm her," he whispered.

Astonished, Bronwen attempted to remove his arms from around her waist. But she could not escape his lips as they found her own. The kiss was soft and warm, melting away her resistance like the sun upon the snow. Before she had time to react, he was striding back down the beach.

Bronwen stood stunned for a moment, clutching his woollen mantle about her. Suddenly she cried out, "Wait, Jacques! Your mantle!"

The dark one turned to her. "Keep it for now," he shouted into the wind. "I shall ask for it when we meet again."

* * * * *

Don't miss this deeply moving
Love Inspired Historical story about
a medieval lady who finds strength in God
to save her family legacy—and to open her heart to love.

THE BRITON
by Catherine Palmer
available February 2008

And also look for
HOMESPUN BRIDE
by Jillian Hart,
where a Montana woman discovers that love
is the greatest blessing of all.

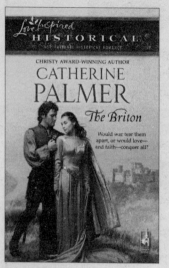

REQUEST YOUR FREE BOOKS!
2 FREE RIVETING INSPIRATIONAL NOVELS
PLUS 2 FREE MYSTERY GIFTS

Love Inspired®
SUSPENSE

YES! Please send me 2 FREE Love Inspired® Suspense novels and my 2 FREE mystery gifts. After receiving them, if I don't wish to receive any more books, I can return the shipping statement marked "cancel." If I don't cancel, I will receive 4 brand-new novels every month and be billed just $3.99 per book in the U.S. or $4.74 per book in Canada, plus 25¢ shipping and handling per book and applicable taxes, if any*. That's a savings of 20% off the cover price! I understand that accepting the 2 free books and gifts places me under no obligation to buy anything. I can always return a shipment and cancel at any time. Even if I never buy another book from Steeple Hill, the two free books and gifts are mine to keep forever.

123 IDN EL5H   323 IDN ELQH

Name	(PLEASE PRINT)	
Address		Apt. #
City	State/Prov.	Zip/Postal Code

Signature (if under 18, a parent or guardian must sign)

Order online at www.LoveInspiredSuspense.com

Or mail to Steeple Hill Reader Service™:

IN U.S.A.: P.O. Box 1867, Buffalo, NY 14240-1867
IN CANADA: P.O. Box 609, Fort Erie, Ontario L2A 5X3

Not valid to current Love Inspired Suspense subscribers.

Want to try two free books from another series?
Call 1-800-873-8635 or visit www.morefreebooks.com

* Terms and prices subject to change without notice. NY residents add applicable sales tax. Canadian residents will be charged applicable provincial taxes and GST. This offer is limited to one order per household. All orders subject to approval. Credit or debit balances in a customer's account(s) may be offset by any other outstanding balance owed by or to the customer. Please allow 4 to 6 weeks for delivery.

Your Privacy: Steeple Hill is committed to protecting your privacy. Our Privacy Policy is available online at www.eHarlequin.com or upon request from the Reader Service. From time to time we make our lists of customers available to reputable firms who may have a product or service of interest to you. If you would prefer we not share your name and address, please check here. ☐

LISUS07

Love Inspired®
SUSPENSE

TITLES AVAILABLE NEXT MONTH

Don't miss these four stories in February

VENDETTA by Roxanne Rustand
Snow Canyon Ranch
After what the McAllisters did to his father, Cole Daniels was determined never to forgive or forget. Then Leigh McAllister landed in danger, and Cole had to decide what was stronger—his old grudge or his need to protect his new chance at love.

MISSING PERSONS by Shirlee McCoy
Reunion Revelations
Lauren Owens had her job and her faith on track, and she looked forward to tackling the mystery back at Magnolia College...until the problem turned deadly. She found herself turning to ex-boyfriend Seth Chartrand for support, for safety and love.

BAYOU CORRUPTION by Robin Caroll
All Alyssa LeBlanc wanted was to distance herself from Lagniappe, Louisiana...and from ace reporter Jackson Devereaux. But once she witnessed the attack on the sheriff, she knew she couldn't walk away. Working with Jackson, Alyssa investigated the crime—and uncovered her past.

LETHAL DECEPTION by Lynette Eason
When guerillas held Cassidy McKnight captive in the Amazon, ex-Navy SEAL turned E.R. doctor Gabe Sinclair returned to his military roots to rescue her. He thought the job was done, yet danger followed Cassidy home....

LISCNM0108